The Border Keeper

THE
BORDER
KEEPER

KERSTIN HALL

A TOM DOHERTY ASSOCIATES BOOK
NEW YORK

THE BORDER KEEPER

Cover art by Kathleen Jennings
Cover design by Christine Foltzer

Edited by Ruoxi Chen

A Tor.com Book
Published by Tom Doherty Associates
120 Broadway
New York, NY 10271

www.tor.com

Tor® is a registered trademark of
Macmillan Publishing Group, LLC.

ISBN 978-1-250-20942-9 (ebook)
ISBN 978-1-250-20941-2 (trade paperback)

First Edition: July 2019

For Tessa

The Border Keeper

Chapter One

SHE LIVED WHERE THE railway tracks met the saltpan, on the Ahri side of the shadowline. In the old days, when people still talked about her, she was known as the end-of-the-line woman.

She had other titles, many more, although most lay forgotten and buried now. Whispers of her presence rustled down through the centuries, a footnote here, a folksong there. Rumours. Myths. Yet she did not dwell in a house of bones, or eat children, or carve hexes into the entrails of men beneath the light of the full autumn moon. In most respects, she appeared no different from other people.

She had been called the destroyer of empires. Mistress of the dead, the whispers went. But those few who knew better gave her the title of yaWenzta, the border keeper.

Her domain was silent. Beyond the fine wire fence of the shadowline, beyond the border of the world, lay Mkalis. The pan stretched white and pitiless to the horizon, a salt heat haze of mirrors, dreams, and thirst. Mkalis, where gods and demons waged endless war for dominion over nine hundred and ninety-nine realms. No Ahri-dweller survived it, not without permissions and a guide.

The border keeper's house might once have been a terminal station, but the trains had stopped running over a hundred years before. Metal tracks blistered with corrosion. The wind buried steel and the sun transformed wood into pale marble, so that from a distance the railway glittered like tarnished jewellery. Fool's gold.

Many would have called Vasethe a fool. Many, in fact, *had*. Yet here he was, walking along the backbone of the desert. His black hair was bound in a loose ponytail, his ear rimmed with silver hoops. A gourd sloshed at his hip. Hidden beneath his shirt, a large tattoo splayed out across his brown shoulders in an illegible tangle of black swirls and switches. His gait gave the impression of easy nonchalance; step roll change, step roll change, and every now and again his fingers would caress the scar that bisected his neck—an ugly white mark like a root or tumour, an underground thing. He did not leave footprints in his wake.

At the end of the tracks, the border keeper's sandstone house shimmered, the walls warping in a liquid haze. All was quiet and bright. A tumbledown fence surrounded the building and, as Vasethe drew nearer, he saw small trinkets strung to the posts. Chains of green-glass beads, cloves stuffed in fine mesh, amputated dolls' legs bound in raffia. They hung on the fence like detritus after a storm.

Vasethe unlatched the gate, making a point to rattle the chain, and stepped inside the yard. Salt crystals crunched beneath his boots. The front door was weathered white with age and heat. Vasethe knocked six times; clear, but not too loud. The temperature was scarcely cooler beneath the tattered awning, and sweat stuck his hair to his neck.

No one answered. The ragged gauze curtains covering the windows remained still.

He did not knock again. After a minute of standing in the doorway, he sighed and rubbed the stubble shading his jaw. Turning away from the door, his eyes fell upon the shale slab sitting below the front window. The fossil of a prehistoric fish swam through the crumbling grey stone. His gaze rose.

The frame of the awning was fixed to the wall at two points, where wooden beams held the wasted canvas taut. The left beam lay above the slab; the right was within reach if he stood on the window ledge and stretched.

The thick twine securing the canvas was encrusted with salt, and resisted efforts to be tugged free. Vasethe's nails splintered, but he worked at the knots until they loosened. He lowered the canvas to the ground.

Exposure had reduced the awning to a gauze-thin layer that tore under the lightest pressure. He probed the canvas with his fingers. Although the outer edges were salvageable, a vast swath in the centre was not.

He cut away this section with a small knife that he kept in his boot, and measured the width of the amputated canvas before setting it aside. The shadow cast by the wall lengthened, but the heat did not abate. Beyond the yard, the flatlands glittered with illusions. The water in Vasethe's canteen ran dry.

He unrolled his sleeping tarp and removed three feet of fabric off the end. Then, with a wicked needle from his pack, he stitched the tarp to the awning. Occasionally, the needle slipped and pierced the skin of his forefinger or thumb, leaving a regular pattern of bloody splotches beside the rows of neat cross-stitches.

Once he had finished, Vasethe stepped onto the shale slab. He restrung the awning so that it sat flush against the wall. Satisfied, he got down and took a seat in the shade to watch the last rays of sunlight disappear behind the horizon.

"Bodies decompose slowly around here."

The voice drifted out of the window. Vasethe did not react; he remained seated, staring out at the desert.

"Bacteria do not thrive in this environment." A key

jangled in the lock and the front door opened. "So, I don't like people dying near my house."

"I wasn't planning on dying," he said.

"Then what are you doing here?"

The woman was smaller than Vasethe had expected; blue-black skin, fierce, with a disconcerting face. Something about the set of her features was odd, but in isolation they seemed ordinary. She wore a grey shift, no shoes, no jewellery, and held herself with a brusque arrogance, like royalty. It was difficult to judge her age.

"Do people often die near your house?" he asked.

"Depends. Not recently."

"I see." Vasethe stood and dusted off his pants. Upright, he was a head taller than the woman in the doorway. He held out his hand. "Pleased to make your acquaintance."

"I'm not. There is blood on your hands."

"They aren't fatal wounds."

For the first time, the expression on her face changed. The corner of her mouth twitched. "The cold will kill you, not blood loss. Out here, exposure is a predator. If not the cold, then dehydration. You have no more water."

"A predicament." He did not sound concerned.

"So, you force me to choose. Do I let you die in my yard and endure the presence of your desiccated remains for decades? Or do I brave your company for the night and then send you on your way?"

"There is a third option."

"Oh, there are more than three, stranger," she said. "For example, I could obliterate you with a snap of my fingers. I could toss you across the shadowline and let the Ageless devour you. I suppose I could even bury you. So many choices, but the first two are the only ones I'm considering right now. Unless you really annoy me, that is."

"Got it."

She sighed and moved aside. A gust of cool air brushed Vasethe's bare arms. "Come in, then."

The interior was dark and sparse. A faded rug dressed the sandy floor, the threads worn to a uniform brown. A mound of battered cushions lay in a heap under the window; a cracked butane lantern hung low from the ceiling.

"What should I call you?" Vasethe asked, eyeing the lantern as he stepped through the door.

"Whatever you want, stranger."

"Will Eris do?"

At the sound of the name, the air shivered. A shadow crossed her face.

"I had hoped that one was forgotten," she muttered.

"Not quite. Not by everybody."

Eris hesitated, then left him standing in the middle of the room as she disappeared into her kitchen.

"My name is Vasethe," he called after her. "I'm glad to finally meet you."

She did not respond.

Vasethe sank into the pile of cushions. Alone, his legs trembled and his muscles went slack. The last phase of his journey had taken five days. Five days with little food or water, following the railway tracks through the desert.

Eris reappeared in the doorway with a tray. She set a chipped ceramic teapot and a single blue cup on the ground beside him. A chain of pink stargazers circled the lip of the cup.

"Drink," she said.

"Thank you."

For a moment longer she appraised him, then returned to her kitchen.

He poured from the pot and breathed in the steam. Cardamom, rooibos. A faint citrus aroma, some irretraceable and familiar scent just beyond his grasp. Too hot to drink; he placed the cup back on the tray to cool.

"Why did you do that?" Her voice floated out of the kitchen.

"Pardon me?"

"You could hardly walk. Why were you renovating my house?"

Vasethe traced the pattern of stargazers with his fingernail. The tiny stigma of the flowers had been gilded in silver. Eris started chopping something; a knife hit the surface of a cutting board in a stream of clicks.

"The fabric had worn through," he said.

"And?"

"It should be more effective now."

"Oh, so I can provide shade to other romantic fools? Fill my yard with their bones?"

"Who said anything about romantic?"

A pause.

"You're all the same. All here to demand miracles."

He drank from his cup. The tea tasted strong and bitter; it stung his throat as he swallowed.

"I'll admit," she continued, "no one has tried to bribe me with household chores before. I commend the novel approach. But I'm much too old to fall for it, stranger."

"How old?"

Oil hissed in a pan.

Vasethe took another sip of his tea, let the warmth spread tendrils inside his chest, and set down the cup. He exhaled.

"I first heard stories about you in a common room at Utyl University," he said. "In those accounts, you were named Wrengreth, Destroyer of the City of Addis Hal Rata, Queen of Snakes."

"The storyteller had poetic tastes, it seems."

"She was reading from *Mish's Compendium*. 'And so

Wrengreth, with hair ablaze and skin dyed scarlet with blood, descended upon Addis Hal Rata, the heart of the 41st realm, home of the Goddess Fanieq, and smote all who lived there, down to the children, the dogs and the rats. And when she roared, the mountains flinched to hear her grief, and the snakes fled their holes to assemble as her army, till all the ground writhed with their reptile flesh.'"

The hissing subsided; Eris had added a liquid into the mix. The smell of onions and turmeric made his mouth water.

"Any truth to the poetry?" he asked.

"I can't say I recall *that* many snakes. You must have an exceptional memory."

He poured himself more tea. "So, you killed the inhabitants of an entire realm?"

"I slaughtered Fanieq and everyone else in my path." She emerged from the kitchen carrying a bowl. "Eat."

He took the bowl from her. "Won't you join me?"

Her teeth flashed. "Most certainly not."

~

A full moon rose over the pan and ghosts whispered in the bright white wideness. The bundle of dolls' legs clattered against the fence.

The woman, the border keeper, once Wrengreth, for now called Eris, held silent conference in the yard. Her arms were held outstretched like wings.

A few feet beyond the yard stood the shadowline. At first inspection, an ordinary fence, if very long—it stretched as far as the eye could see. Not especially sturdy, just four wires strung to wooden posts, reaching only thigh-high.

But on closer investigation, the strangest property of the fence became apparent. Although the moon's glow illuminated the yard, the house, and Eris, light did not reflect from the wires or the posts. The entire fence remained a uniform black, as if dipped in pitch. It did not cast a shadow on either side.

Vasethe gazed out over the scene. He was about to lie down and go back to sleep, when it materialised.

It did not seem to cross distance; there was nothing to preface its arrival. He blinked, and the creature appeared. It stood perhaps a hundred paces from the shadowline.

Eris flinched.

The creature was taller than a man but thin and mangled, like an ancient desert tree flayed by the salt wind. It was missing its right leg, balanced only on the left. Bone gleamed; part of the creature's skull was visible where the blackened skin had peeled away. The rest of its face remained shadowed. It gave the impression of unsteadiness, like it was poised to fall.

It did not move. It just stood there. Watching.

The dolls' legs rattled furiously, the glass beads clinked against one another, but Eris held still. Vasethe watched her a while longer, then lay down and slept.

Chapter Two

CLOSE TO THE SHADOWLINE, temperatures only cycled between extremes. Darkness was frozen and light blistering.

When night dropped away, the heat took its place. Warmth melted the frost that beaded the handle of the water bucket beside the well; it hit the sand, hit the walls, hit the tracks.

"Stranger." Eris's voice had a dangerous edge.

Vasethe sat on the shale slab beneath the awning, polishing his boots with a rag. He had recovered since the evening before; his skin had lost its ashen pallor and his eyes were sharp and alert.

"Yes?"

"What have you done to my floor?"

Eris had returned to the house after midnight. Vasethe feigned sleep when she passed him, had heard her unsteady breathing.

"I'm not sure what you are referring to." He tried to look worried, failed. "Have I damaged it?"

"You washed it."

"Nonsense." He resumed buffing his boot. "When would I have had time for that?"

"I can only imagine during the early hours of this morning."

He folded the rag and tucked it into a pocket in his pack, then stretched his legs. "Are you offended?"

"I haven't decided yet." She crossed her arms. "I'm trying to work out how you swept and washed the floor without waking me."

"Quietly."

"I'm a light sleeper."

"Very quietly." Vasethe stood up. Eris hung in the doorway, watching him. Guardedly. With interest. "I used your well. I take it that it endlessly refills itself? Like your teapot?"

"Who are you, stranger?"

"No one really. I've been a scholar, a cook in a bar, a messenger, worked a brief stint as a priest, shafei herder, even shorter stint as a tailor's assistant . . ."

"Your point?"

"There isn't all that much to me."

"And now?"

"On a hiatus."

"It's a strange place to rest." Eris stared out at the shimmering tracks. They stretched towards the indistinct horizon, swallowed by heat and distance.

Vasethe followed her gaze. "I should be going."

"What did you study?"

"I was never particularly focussed, to be honest. I started out in medicine and got distracted by history and linguistics."

"I see."

"Thank you for your hospitality." He held out his hand. Eris did not take it.

"Is something wrong?"

"It's been a long time," she said, "since I last had company. Since adopting this body, I haven't spoken to anyone."

He lowered his hand.

"Stay," she said, as if the idea had just occurred to her. "For one more day. I want to know what's happening in the rest of Ahri."

She disappeared into the house.

A faint smile crossed Vasethe's face. He followed her into the clean room and set his pack down. Although Eris had not noticed, he had also washed the gauze curtains and cushions. The room was perceptibly brighter and smelled of soap.

She fetched a spool of leather cording and wad of black feathers from her bedroom. While Vasethe spoke, she knotted the them together.

He started broad. He described the escalating tensions

between Utyl and Rabri Uhm, the rise and fall of empresses, the routing of terrors from Feki Road. He drew a pad of crumpled paper from his pack, and sketched while he spoke, illustrating his stories with rough caricatures and drafts of landscapes.

Her interest in major world events proved secondary to her desire for the particulars; she hungered for the smaller details of ordinary lives. She wanted to know what people valued, their songs and fireside stories, customs, their individual tragedies and triumphs, feelings. Vasethe told her about rain festivals and initiation rituals, the strange superstitions held by inhabitants of the volcanic isles in the far north, self-proclaimed necromancers of the western gambling towns, villages of children. He described the great libraries of Utyl, Kwasa's famed harbour, the crystal caves of Pol. All the while, he spoke with an insider's knowledge but never about himself.

Eris completed her feathered ward and set it aside. Her wariness faded by degrees. She offered the occasional contribution of her own, about the nomads who used to occupy Chenash, or about long-dead travellers from Jiksem or Phon who had knocked on her door in years past. She joked about their prowess in bed.

The sun moved across the sky and they migrated to the kitchen. A furrowed wooden table took up most of the space, surrounded by three rickety chairs. Eris opened the door to her pantry and brought out handfuls of peaches and bright peppers. She set them down on the table. Later, when she opened the pantry a second time, Vasethe saw that more had replaced those taken.

While he spoke, she pitted the peaches and basted them in cinnamon, thyme, and pomegranate molasses. Vasethe cut the peppers and scraped away the tiny white seeds. He recounted the intrigue surrounding the assassination of the crown prince of Pol, laying out the factions and rumours. The light fell; Eris lit a candle and roasted the peaches in her oven. When the fruit turned brown, she emptied the oven tray into a single bowl and gave it to Vasethe. She started searing the peppers with a handful of brown grains and cashew nuts.

The dolls' legs rattled.

Vasethe stopped speaking midsentence. With a soft hiss, the fire inside the stove went out and the kitchen was suddenly quiet and cold. *Clack, clack, clack,* the wooden legs hit the post.

Eris flowed out of the room, gone in an instant. The candle flame wavered and died.

Vasethe got up and took the skillet off the stovetop. Through the window he could see the wards trembling along the yard's fence, their clattering loud in the stillness. The moon gleamed above the southern horizon. He leaned over and checked the knife in his boot.

She stood in the middle of the yard, perfectly still, staring out at the saltpan beyond the shadowline. Her back was to Vasethe. He watched her from beneath the deeper shadows of the awning.

As before, it appeared without warning. Much closer this time, only a few paces from the line. The creature's eyes were the colour of old milk left in the sun. It gazed unblinkingly at Eris.

A moment later Vasethe saw the second creature, farther off, trailing its brother.

The moon rose. Like a children's game, no one moved while they were watched. The creatures' presence radiated through the cold air, keen-edged and contaminated.

Then, as abruptly as they appeared, they were gone. The wards stilled. Vasethe let out a long, slow breath.

A shiver ran across the border keeper's shoulders, the first movement she had made since the creatures appeared.

"Eris?" Vasethe called.

"Don't say that name." Her voice was like the wind over dead leaves.

He stepped out into the moonlight. "Are you . . ."

"Four hundred years. Then you arrive and it starts again." Eris turned. Her cheeks were wet, and her eyes shone bright and furious. The air crackled with power. "Why?"

He stumbled backwards. "I don't know."

She took a step towards him and his knees buckled. Blood trickled from his nose.

"I don't know," he gasped. Pressure pounded against his chest in waves; he struggled to speak. "But I'm sorry. I'm sorry."

A moment longer. Then the pressure abated. Vasethe sagged back onto his heels, breathing heavily.

"I will take you to Mkalis."

There was blood in his mouth. He raised his head to look at her.

"I will find out what you want and who you are and then I will destroy you."

"I—"

"What was her name, the dead woman you loved?"

He shook his head.

Eris gestured, a quick twist of her wrist, and Vasethe flew backwards. The air left his lungs as he slammed into the ground.

"Her *name*."

"You don't understand." He coughed, clutching his ribs. Eris walked closer, each footfall a threat.

"But I will. No more lies. Tell me the name of your woman."

The desert fell quiet; the whole world held its breath.

"Raisha," Vasethe whispered.

Chapter Three

ALL WAS AMBER BEYOND THE HOUSE, the late afternoon seeping into evening.

Vasethe waited in the yard. A slight frown creased his forehead. On the fence, the new ward hung like a feathered star.

Inside, Eris stalked circles around the front room and muttered to herself. She had not spoken since the night before, and Vasethe had kept his distance. As she paced, the hair on his arms rose. Whatever she was weaving, it was powerful.

The dryness of the saltpan had left his lips cracked and swollen. He ran his finger over the rough skin and his frown deepened.

"Enter," commanded Eris.

The floor inside the room glowed with a faint purple light. In the corners of Vasethe's vision, vague shapes moved through lazy spirals.

"I'm going to perform a questing. It will reveal the location of your woman," Eris said. "When that's done, I'll find a vessel for you. Unlike me, your soul is single-aspected, so you won't be able to move through Mkalis without a surrogate form to house your consciousness."

Vasethe nodded.

"Sit. Novices tend to become disorientated."

He moved to where she indicated. Eris took up position opposite him and extended her hands to touch his knees.

"This shouldn't be difficult," she said. "Picture the person you are looking for. Hold their smell, image, touch, voice in your mind. Whatever you remember most clearly about them, think of that now. I'll do the rest."

"I think we should talk about this."

"I'm giving you what you came for, so stop wasting my time." The whites of her eyes darkened to black. "Close your eyes, stranger."

Vasethe scowled and did as he was told. Eris's lips moved through unvoiced syllables.

The light of the floor strengthened and turned red. Around them, the walls dissolved into a haze of bloody shadows, and the sky above gleamed like pewter. Eris leaned closer to Vasethe, closing her hands around his wrists. He opened his eyes.

"Strange," she muttered.

The passing silhouettes of huge birds threw deeper shadows across the scene.

"Does this tell you where we need to go?" Vasethe

asked, twisting to see what lay behind him. Massive animals, rolling indistinctly through maroon fog. The clank of chains, the crunching of wheels, growing louder. Strange far-off cries.

"It's disconnected," she murmured, "which can't be right; rulers always have connections. And yet . . ."

A powerful metallic smell, boiled coins or a bubbling crucible, rose from the ground. Vasethe jerked his hands free and found his feet. The scene evaporated like mist and the room reappeared, orange and cool.

"Why did you do that?" Eris asked, tilting her head to one side.

Vasethe swallowed. His hands were slick with cold sweat. "Sorry, I didn't realise I would break the connection. Should we try again?"

"No need." Eris's eyes retained their curious light, even as the whites resumed their usual colour. "I know roughly where she is, and I can use you to track her the rest of the way. Like a compass."

Relief was plain on Vasethe's face. "Thank you," he said.

"You're in luck, actually," she said. "It seems that your lover is in a realm with a negligible population, which will make finding her easier. I'm not sure who the realm belongs to, but they have a tenuous connection to Kan Buyak. I've dealt with him in the past; he's a bastard but largely harmless. We'll need to traverse his realm to acquire permissions to enter theirs."

"When can we begin?"

"Eager?" Eris stood and smoothed her clothes. "Have something to eat. I'll find a vessel for you."

"If the Ageless return tonight, will your wards be enough to hold them?"

Eris's fingers twitched. "Don't worry; my wards are enough, unless the whole contingent makes an appearance." Her lip curled. "Leave me before I change my mind."

Vasethe gave her a mocking bow and backed into the kitchen. Once out of her sight, his hands began to shake. He opened her cupboards and crouched to inspect the lower shelves. A couple of black bottles with peeling labels, some of the corks rotted through. He opened a muscatel and took a deep swig. The sweet, cutting wine spread warmth down his scarred throat.

He stopped shaking.

Sounds of movement drifted out from Eris's bedroom, a part of the house he had not yet trespassed. He found her rummaging through her closet. Of all the rooms in the house, this was the only one to hint at any kind of sentimentality. A battered stuffed rabbit flopped over the top of the wardrobe and a paper-crisp orchid stood in a glass vase on her writing desk. Dead and frozen in time.

An old painting hung opposite the foot of her bed, capturing a waterfall beneath autumn trees. Although the colours had faded, the edges of leaves still glowed gold, and the spray was pale and diffuse. Every time she woke up, she would see that painting, and judging by the dust coating the frame, it had hung there for a very long time.

"Here." Eris tossed Vasethe a black bundle of velvet. He caught it.

"A blindfold?"

"You are familiar with them?" She raised an eyebrow.

He chose not to reply, running a finger along the edge of the musty ribbon.

She sighed and returned to the closet. "There are a few special threads woven into the seam. They will allow me to find you in the event that we are separated. They also help to calm nerves."

"I'm not nervous."

"You should be." With a grunt, she pulled a crate from the back of the wardrobe and set it on the ground. "Just wear it."

"As you wish."

"Exactly. Lie down."

"Here?"

"*Yes*, here."

He sidled around her, eying the line of intimacy he

needed to cross. Eris was delving into the crate, oblivious to his discomfort. Vasethe sat on the corner of her rumpled, unmade bed. Her sheets were yellow with age.

She lifted a bone-handled ice pick, held it up to the light to check its sharpness. "How much do you know about Mkalis?"

"Follow the rules, get consent, don't eat or drink."

"And about crossing?"

"Less."

She snorted. "That's fine; I'll do it for you. For Buyak, the most important realm rule is to always speak the truth. Opinions are fine as long as you phrase them with care, but no figurative language and no lying. This will be difficult for you, so I'd recommend speaking as little as possible."

He smiled.

"Follow my lead and we'll pass through his realm within a night." She straightened. "Buyak shouldn't pay us any heed; much too busy with social warfare."

"Social warfare?"

"He's a schemer," she said. "Ruthlessly ambitious, impeccably polite. Which brings me to rule two: Trust no one beyond the shadowline. The rulers will kill you for sport; the dwellers are little better."

"*You* intend to kill me."

"Yes, but at a specific and agreed-upon time."

"I don't remember agreeing."

"Well, you can't have everything," she said. "Lie down, stranger."

He shifted backwards on the mattress. Although dishevelled, her bed smelt like oasis flowers and lingering warmth.

"You appear tense," Eris said, with wry amusement. "Are you sure you aren't nervous?"

"To be fair, that is a sharp implement in your hands."

She twirled the pick between her fingers. It caught the gleam of the butane lantern through the doorway. "Put on the blindfold."

Vasethe lay back, tying the blindfold behind his head. The heavy velvet blocked all light; he could see nothing. He was suddenly aware of his own breathing, of the small sounds of Eris moving, his pulse. He flinched when she touched his jaw.

"Open your mouth," she said.

"Why?"

"No questions."

Blood burnt his tongue, the salt drops scalding his mouth. He choked, surprised, and tried to sit up, but Eris pressed a hand flat on his chest.

"Stay still," she said.

"Eris, what—you're bleeding."

"Time for you to fall asleep, stranger."

"What is going on?" He reached for the blindfold, but she restrained him.

"Hush," she whispered.

"Why is it so hot?" he slurred.

"Don't ask so many questions."

"Witch's blood—acid?"

Her nails dug into his skin. "Of course it isn't, you imbecile."

"Burning . . ." he murmured. Bright yellow stars darted across his vision. "I can't move."

"That's the idea."

She said something else, but he could not understand the words.

Chapter Four

VASETHE'S EYES REMAINED CLOSED, and yet he could see.

He lay on Eris's bed. He also stood on a hillside beneath a sky of wispy clouds, long platinum grass grazing his knees. Rose-coloured spheres bobbed overhead like giant dandelion heads, and craggy ironstone mountains hemmed the western horizon.

His body had changed too; his hands were unscarred and his skin a few shades lighter than in Ahri. Younger, this new body; within it he felt unbalanced. He wore a high-collared vest, like those favoured by the courtiers of the Pol Imperial Assembly, and loose green pants. His boots, however, were reassuringly similar to his usual pair.

"Eris?"

His voice emerged hoarse. Vasethe touched his throat. Wet. An oily yellow liquid glistened on his fingertips. The wound on his throat—long-healed and scarred over—had reopened, and the blistering, swollen gash festered with infection.

And yet, this vessel was *not* his body. This wound had no right to exist in Mkalis.

Something small and wriggling dropped from the gash and squirmed into the grass. He grimaced and crushed the maggot beneath his heel.

"Eris?" he called again, louder.

Far-off laughter. He turned on the spot and scanned the landscape. No one. At the base of the hill, the vegetation thickened where a copse of trees filled the valley.

He made his way down the slope through the rustling grass and the pungent smell of vanilla rose from the soil. The spheres rotated slowly.

Down the hill and into the valley. Something about this place reminded him of a children's song, or a holy chant, but he could not remember what came next. There was a part about a house, and hidden waters, but no, that still wasn't quite it. A thin path led into the shadows beneath the silver-leaved trees, and sweet yellow blossoms bordered the trail, petals shining in the dappled light.

A dull sense of dread had settled in his bones. Familiar. He knew this place, yet when he tried to grasp the memory, it dissolved into darkness.

He needed to find Eris.

The trees grew denser, closer, more secretive. Darker. Vasethe kept his steps feather-light and made no sound. The breeze carried a faint odour, like overripe fruit, but more foul, sweeter. Leaves trembled and then fell still.

The sound of running footsteps in the trees behind him, gone in seconds. Silence again. Vasethe's breathing came sharp and fast. A bird sang in the distance, serenading the evening. He stood for a moment, listening. The small grove he had seen from the hillside had warped into a forest of glinting steel leaves and grasping boughs. Roots curled up from the earth at the base of the tree trunks, ink-black and sticky with an oozing residue.

On the other side of the saltpan, beyond the shadowline, Vasethe moaned aloud.

Up ahead, a gap in the trees beckoned. He stepped over a tangle of roots and his heel struck stone. The cobbles were so overgrown that Vasethe could hardly see them through their coating of soft dark moss.

Down the hill and into the valley, where the sun cannot shine, down the hill and into the valley . . .

The words of the song looped over and over in his mind, wheeling out of reach.

The trees parted. In the centre of the wild, weed-choked clearing stood a ramshackle stonewall house. The windows were boarded up on the ground floor, the front door shut tight. Ivy crawled the sagging walls. On the wide porch, a swing seat creaked back and forth, as if someone had just gotten up from it.

Vasethe circled the house, keeping close to the tree

line. The roof was steep and tiled, a soot-stained chimney visible above yellowed gables. Built for colder climates, he thought. Out of place here.

Straggly grass rambled across the yard, snarled with devil-thorns and brambles. A crumbling well sagged beside the rear wall of the house. He leaned over the edge but could not see the bottom. He dropped a pebble. It clattered against dry stone.

When Vasethe rounded the side of the house again, the front door stood ajar. Like a sly smile, an invitation. He hesitated, then climbed the steps up to the porch. The door knocker, shaped like a lion's head, grinned at him from beneath a layer of orange rust.

He pushed the door. It creaked and swung open.

The house's exterior had suggested a rundown cottage, but inside it looked more like a manor. A glass chandelier hung above a wide staircase, cobwebs draped over the candles like streamers. Yellowed wallpaper curled from the skirting boards. Vasethe allowed his eyes to adjust to the gloom before he stepped inside.

"Eris?"

His skin prickled. He walked through the door on the left into a shadowed parlour. Dust coated every surface; this place must have stood abandoned for years. From the wall above the fireplace, a painted hare watched him with wide black eyes. Four wingback chairs faced one another around a squat table. Their orientation struck him as oddly conspiratorial.

The front door locked with a click.

Vasethe froze for a second, then moved towards the boarded-up window. Thick wood, but rotten, holed by termites. Dull evening light filtered through the cracks. If he hit the boards hard enough, they should break off. He made no effort to be quiet now, and the floor groaned under his weight as he examined the rest of the room.

A shushing sound from the foyer—silk sliding over skin, flesh stripping from bone. A sound that was meant to be heard.

Vasethe stepped through the adjoining door into a derelict study. Books were scattered across the floor. They gathered in mounds of folded spines and torn pages, and the shelves lining the walls were bare. In the midst of the chaos hunkered a mahogany desk. A message was scrawled across its dusty surface.

A single word. Impossible, ancient, compound, invented, a secret joke loaded with affection and unspoken yearnings, a parting gift. The word on the desk matched stroke for stroke the tattoo inked across Vasethe's shoulders. A tattoo that wasn't on the shoulders of his surrogate body.

He strode to the desk and wiped away the word, sending dust spiralling through the dim air. Behind him, he thought he heard stifled laughter, but when he spun around, the study was empty. The maggots squirmed in his throat.

He left the study and returned to the foyer.

The stairs leading to the upper floor sagged in the centre, the woven runner brown. He walked on the margin of the staircase. Although the wood groaned and squeaked with every step, it held firm beneath him.

The second-floor landing grew brighter when he reached the top of the stairs. Drab portraits hung on the walls. All of the same child, and in each painting, some part of the canvas had been cut away, amputating legs, arms, gouging out eyes, punctuating the torso with holes. Vasethe's eyes narrowed. The smile of the armless boy mocked him.

Ahead, a faint but regular creaking. The sound grew louder as he made his way down the passage. Most the doors on this floor gaped wide open, except for two at the far end of the corridor. He passed shadowed bedrooms, a sewing room with an ancient spinning wheel, another smaller study overlooking the trees. The lines of portraits stood to silent attention. The creaking grew louder.

The nursery had been blue once, but the paint had flaked away to reveal yellow plaster beneath, with darker ripples of ochre marking seasons of dampness. The cradle rocked and rocked and rocked, empty. Vasethe brought it to a gentle stop with one hand. The house fell quiet once more.

When he turned, he saw the scratches scored into the wood around the door frame. Carved by claws. Or fingernails. The grooves ran deep. He glanced back at the cot, then left the nursery.

Pain seared through Vasethe's throat, but as he reached up to touch the wound, the sensation vanished.

He exhaled, disorientated and faintly nauseous. The last door waited. His hand closed on the cold handle, and he pushed it open.

The woman lay on a four-poster bed, arms crossed over her chest like a corpse. Her dress was clean and white and long, her feet bare, her hair in a single silver braid. A window above the bed illuminated the room in wan starlight, and the light was strongest around her face. Her eyes were open and fixed on him.

"Remember me?" She smiled.

The creaking of the cradle started again.

Vasethe shook his head, although his expression was troubled. "No."

"Historians have short memories," she said.

"I've never seen your face before." He shook his head again, but his nagging sense of anxiety persisted. "Where is the border keeper?"

"I must confess, I feel a little torn." Her smile widened, splitting the corners of her mouth. Blood trickled down her chin. "I hate you, and yet I'm delighted that you're here."

"The border keeper," he pressed.

"Such a good dog, hm? She's coming, which means we'll have to cut this short. No matter; you're already where I want you."

He stared at her. "Dog? Why—"

His throat burned, a brief burst of pain. He clutched his neck.

"Does that hurt?" The flesh of her cheeks gaped raw and fleshy. "Does it hurt, Vasethe?"

Wood splintered against wood with an almighty crack, and the floor beneath him gave way. The bed slid towards him and the woman was smiling, bleeding, smiling, and then he fell, grasping at nothing. The house swallowed him.

Air roared past his ears, the world a shadowed blur. Vasethe hit the ground.

His tibia snapped with the sound of a door slamming closed. He screamed. The splintered bone jutted out from his skin and blood gushed, soaking his leg in warmth.

Far above, something moved. Air left Vasethe's mouth in ragged gasps. The world turned red, white, and black; incomprehensible shapes swam before him.

He gritted his teeth and squeezed his eyes shut, forcing his mind to work. The basement. He had fallen from the second floor into the basement. He coughed and struggled to sit upright. Grit pattered down from the hole in the ceiling.

He used a broken beam to lever himself into an awkward crouch, breathing through his teeth. A skull crunched beneath his foot. They were everywhere, ancient and gleaming and delicate as eggshells, carpeting the basement floor. Everything had a slick coating of black residue, the same oil that had seeped from the roots of the trees. It stuck to Vasethe's hands, leached through the gaps between his fingers. He tried to stand, but dizziness overcame him and he collapsed.

Laughter, the sound of running footsteps.

Vasethe's neck erupted in agony, drowning out the pain of his broken leg in a white-hot flare. He thrashed, clawing at his throat, unable to think, unable to breathe, every nerve in his body alight. The bones beneath him fractured and disintegrated; sharp edges sliced through his shirt, drew blood.

The pain receded. When the world slid back into focus, he could hear someone was in the basement with him. He coughed, shuddering, his neck throbbing with every heartbeat. The person moved towards him quickly, crushing skulls beneath their heels.

"I am here now," Eris said. "Wake up."

Chapter Five

HE TOOK A LONG time to wake, floating in nothingness. No thoughts, no feeling, suspended in the dark.

Her hand rested on his chest, just below his heart. That was the first thing he felt.

Vasethe heaved for air.

A heartbeat later, Eris opened her eyes and pushed herself upright. "Vasethe, listen to me. Focus."

The world shimmered. He could see the walls of the basement, feel the splintered bone stabbed through his skin, the black residue drowning him.

"Focus!" Eris insisted, gripping his arm with painful force.

He was whole and unhurt, he was broken and hunted, he was whole again. Eris disappeared, phantoms flitted across his vision, colours flickered.

"You must drink." A cup knocked against his teeth. He tried to swat it away; *do not eat the food of Mkalis, you shall be trapped, you shall dwell forever in thrall, you shall . . .*

"Drink!"

Eris forced his mouth open. Tea scorched his tongue. He choked.

"Keep drinking."

Vasethe swallowed and reality slowly solidified around him. Eris removed the cup, refilled it, tried to press it into his limp hand. With effort, he sat up, leaning against the headboard for support. He felt sick, and turned his face away when she offered him the cup again.

"Food and drink will anchor you," she said.

"It's hot," he muttered.

"If you can complain, you can drink."

Vasethe's hands shook. He grimaced.

"I'll do it." Eris took the cup back and held it to his mouth.

"Sorry." He drank. The ghostly pains at his throat and shin faded. He closed his eyes, flashes of the nightmare replaying across the lids.

Eris sat back with a sigh. "Well, that went badly."

"What happened?"

She frowned. "I located the corpse in Kan Vanailin's domain, where I planned to start our journey. Vanailin's gateway to Buyak's realm comes out right beside the capital; it should have been easy."

He groaned. "Corpse?"

"What, did you think I was going to build you a vessel out of clay? Be grateful it's fresh."

He tried not to think about his new body. "What went wrong?"

"I'm not sure. I think the vessel was pulled from Vanailin's realm when your consciousness made contact with it. You ended up in an obscure minor realm that I didn't recognise. No border restrictions, though, and it had a gateway to Buyak's domain, so I carried you through while you were unconscious." She stood up, hesitated. "Before I arrived, did you see anyone?"

He slowly shook his head.

"Strange." She seemed distracted. "Never mind. You need to eat. I'll make you food, but keep drinking, as much as you can manage."

He nodded. "Thank you."

"Hm. It's nothing."

"I meant for saving me."

"Drink your tea."

Once he was alone, Vasethe felt his throat. Smooth scar tissue. He rubbed the mark absentmindedly and drank more tea. When he glanced down, he found that his cup was no emptier. The taste of old leaves was acrid in his mouth; he set aside the cup.

The room had darkened, everything reduced to orange-rimmed silhouettes against the glow of the lantern. For a while he lay there, thinking. Then he swung his legs over the edge of the bed and stood.

The room veered sharply and Vasethe staggered as his head spun. He braced himself against the wardrobe and waited for the wave of dizziness to pass.

He found Eris seated on a chair in the kitchen, her head and arms resting on the table. She snored softly. A pot simmered on the stove, and the fragrance of baking bread mingled with the smells of herbs, vegetables, and paprika.

Vasethe checked the flatbread in the oven. He went to the pantry and retrieved the opened bottle of muskatel, setting it on the table. The soup was a warm brown, dotted with dark green flecks of thyme and sage, the transparent curves of onions. He stirred it, tasted, added black pepper, found a lemon, and squeezed its juice into the mix.

Eris started from her doze. She opened her mouth, then shook her head.

"You were a cook once," she said.

He nodded. "I worked in a bar in the docks of Naiké. Not that the fishermen were all that interested in fine dining."

"Your legs are shaking."

"I must be cold."

"You nearly died."

He adjusted the pot. "Is that what happens if the surrogate body is destroyed?"

She sighed. "Not exactly, but you wouldn't wake up."

"So, I'd take even longer to decay." He stirred and then offered a spoonful of soup to her.

She shook her head again. "I don't eat or drink."

"More credit to your cooking, then."

"Stranger, sit down."

He returned to the stove.

"You are infuriating."

"So I have been told."

They did not speak for a while. Vasethe lifted the pot off the heat and ladled a portion of the soup into a bowl, took a tumbler out of the cupboard, and retrieved the bread. Eris poured muskatel into his glass.

"Why don't you eat?" he asked, taking the tumbler from her.

"Not possible. It would lay down roots, compromise my status as the border keeper. I can't be aligned with either Mkalis or Ahri." She watched him drink. "I'm dual-souled; I have bodies on both sides of the shadowline. If I feed the one, the other starves. So, I don't eat or drink. Anywhere."

"That's sad."

"It is?"

"I think so," he nodded. "You've never tasted cherries?"

She smiled and raised her head from the table. "That's specific."

"Or new tide clams in butter? You've never been drunk?" He inclined the tumbler towards her.

"I'm afraid not."

"Doesn't that make you sad?"

She gazed out the window. The stars gleamed on the railway tracks, and she was quiet for a while.

"If you live a long time, small, passing things hold less weight," she said.

Vasethe rested his spoon in the bowl. The silence stretched. Eris kept staring out the window and her voice was low and flat.

"I remember my deaths," she said. "The first few are clear, and the latest ones. Those in between can be hazy, but some days I wake up and the memory of a half-forgotten dying hits me, and I think, 'That person is gone.'" She shook her head. "So, no, life without cherries isn't nearly as painful as you would think."

He broke a corner off the flatbread and dipped it in the soup. "Do you think of your incarnations as different people?"

"I guess, although it's more complex than that. My vessels have their individual quirks, but all of us hold old memories. And old feelings."

"So, 'Eris' is the name of a dead woman?"

She smiled slightly. "Five hundred years dead. But you already knew that."

"I didn't."

She cocked her head to one side. He shook his head and drank.

"Then why did you choose it?"

"Is it true that you were once known as Midan, Lord and Defender of Ydrithano, favourite of the God-King Yett?"

She leaned back in her chair and waited.

Vasethe sighed. "Okay. An answer for an answer. Agreed?"

She lowered her head in acquiescence.

"I made a promise which led me here. The person I made the promise to called you 'Eris.'"

Her brow furrowed. "That raises more questions than it answers. Very well. Yes, I was Midan and all the rest. I can adopt male bodies, if there are no willing girl children around. I just prefer not to."

"That wasn't the source of my curiosity, to be honest."

"Oh?"

Vasethe pushed the bowl away and sat back. "You fell in love with a god."

Her eyes narrowed. "And?"

"How was that?"

"Good. Until it wasn't."

"Until his death?"

"Until his *murder.* Why are you stirring this up?"

"And you went from Midan to Wrengreth?"

"*An* answer for *an* answer, stranger. Where did you hear of Midan?"

He rubbed his eyes. "Okay, okay. I studied history. My research delved into the role of the border keeper in post–Demon War treaty negotiations. So I'm familiar with some of your more famous incarnations."

She stared. "You *studied* me?"

"I studied historical accounts, which may have been inaccurate. Probably inaccurate."

"I take it back: I would give a *lot* for a drink. Although I suppose it explains how—"

The wards stirred against the fence outside. They both stiffened.

Eris placed a finger to her lips and stood. She left the kitchen without haste and Vasethe stayed slumped on the kitchen chair. The rattling of the wards grew louder. For the first time, he could hear another sound below it—a deep grinding noise, rising and falling in volume.

He got up and joined Eris in the yard.

The Ageless had increased in number. The first two stood sentinel a few steps from the line. The third had no jawbone, and its torso was riddled with ragged, coin-sized holes. It stood perhaps fifty yards behind its siblings, frozen in mid-step.

Vasethe sat down on the shale slab beside the door

and pulled the knife from his boot. He laid it across his lap. Then he leaned against the wall and waited, while the bright moon tracked its course across the sky and the wards chattered and the railway tracks shone.

Chapter Six

ERIS DID NOT SUGGEST crossing to Mkalis again and Vasethe did not ask. She now held him at a wary, oscillating length, at times cold and at others curious. While she made her mind up about him, Vasethe endeavoured to be helpful.

Although he stayed out of her bedroom, the kitchen and yard were fair game. He scrubbed the stove and refitted the oven door so that it no longer sagged from its hinges. The pantry was emptied, dusted, rearranged, restacked. The taps were polished, the drains cleared, the chairs fixed. Over the course of several mornings, the kitchen was transformed.

The butane lantern presented more of a problem. He could not repair cracked glass, so he needed to replace the damaged pane. Unfortunately, this meant bringing up the subject with Eris.

"You do realise I could stamp my foot and this place would transform into a palace?" she said.

Nevertheless, she directed him to the basement storeroom, the entrance a trapdoor at the rear of the house.

The heat hung in the air like a heavy curtain. Vasethe hesitated before descending into the cool, dark underground. The memory of a rocking cradle lingered in his mind.

Decades of accumulated dust covered crates and boxes, and he sneezed. Eris had left a lumpy wax candle at the base of the stairs. He lit it and surveyed his options.

Although the storeroom was cramped and decrepit, determining exactly where the walls were proved difficult. No matter which way Vasethe turned, the space before him was always larger than expected, the edges just beyond the candle's reach.

He found a pile of Atvanian burl walnut, the wood buried beneath jars of pickled vegetables and shafei fur coats. Books teetered on high stacks, well-read tomes written in alphabets long forgotten. Paintings and sketches—lovely or ugly—were treated with equal neglect.

Porcelain figurines, predominantly waterfowl, with their heads snapped off. Priceless Ebri jewellery, the relics of a lost civilisation, draped over coral from the Xet Gulf. Untouched manuscripts from Utyl University on the topics of skin necrosis and Pol etiquette, on haemomancy and the extinct lizards of Chenash.

He also found a number of lanterns. Some ordinary, some crafted from materials unfamiliar to him. One shaped from grape-coloured gel, another from greenish bone.

When he emerged from the storeroom, grey with dust and pleased, Vasethe held a small brass lantern. The panes were black with soot but it was whole and suitable.

He sat on the rock under the awning. It took time to scrub away the layers of grime, revealing rose glass panes, delicate filigree catches. He loosened his shoulders and his face relaxed.

Once his prize was spotless, Vasethe took down the old lantern and replaced it with the new. Evening fell; the Pearl Star appeared in the southeast, solitary in the vastness above, and the front room glowed pink and warm.

"Didn't your mother tell you not to rub old lamps?" Eris asked grumpily.

Vasethe sat in the corner on his freshly laundered cushions and fell asleep scheming.

In the dark morning chill, he returned to the basement. The walnut beams were heavy, and getting the wood out through the trapdoor took effort. As the sun emerged above the horizon, the wood grew golden and rich with honeyed whorls. Already sweating, Vasethe hunted through the storeroom until he found an array of tools: saws and chisels, hammers and screws.

He measured lengths, sawed, and squared off the beams. The grain of the wood felt like velvet beneath his hands and smelled of distant forests, earthy and drenched in rain.

The sun blasted the desert. Vasethe shed his shirt and kept working.

He cut hidden notches and keys into the work peices, sanded and smoothed so that the parts slid together as cleanly as an oiled lock. As he set each new piece into place, he double-checked that the top plane remained level. His process was methodical. He rarely looked up from his craft and his movements had a practiced quality, muscles familiar with the heft of the materials.

The tea table was a comfortable size and height, simple and heavy. Vasethe stretched his shoulders and stood. Drawing a bucket of water from the well, he doused himself. It did not take long for him to dry, the sun leeching moisture from his clothes.

Eris stood in the doorway and watched him.

"Carpentry?"

He shook out his damp hair, then gathered it into a ponytail. "One of my first occupations."

"You must be older than you look, to have practised so many professions."

"Or I'm a quick learner." He winked.

Eris gave him a hard look. He lifted the table with a soft grunt, placing it beneath the shade of the awning.

"I can't trust you," she said.

"That's unfortunate."

"You put on a good show, though."

"A show?" He crouched down beside the table.

"Absolutely." She sighed. "I haven't survived as the border keeper without instincts, and you are not what you seem."

Vasethe ran his hands over the top of the table, considering his words. "Maybe. I don't lie very often. But there are things I haven't told you. Personal, insignificant things."

"Insignificant?"

"To the great and all-powerful border keeper of the shadowline, yes."

"Are you mocking me?"

"Wouldn't dream of it," he said, although his voice was smiling. He picked up a chisel.

Eris fell silent but did not leave. She rubbed her calf muscle, using her left foot.

"You're dangerous," she said at last.

"Debatable."

She sat down on the doorstep. "I find your tattoo confusing. Is it supposed to read as 'dog of any master'?"

"You recognise traditional Gislapur."

"But it's more than that." She frowned. "It has elements of other languages, or at least some kind of back-country dialect. Why would you have an insult written in a dead language on your back?"

Vasethe selected a different chisel and set about carving a finer detail. He brushed away a curl of walnut.

"And I assume the misspelling was intentional. 'Dog' would be pronounced correctly as 'tse,' but it's a homophone. The pictograph has been altered here; the radical for 'animal' is written as 'true' or 'sincere.'"

"I have known scholars who would cut off their own limbs for your knowledge."

"It turns the phrase into a paradox. 'Dog of any master' refers to a disloyal beast. But 'true'?" She shook her head. "I can't say I understand the intention behind it."

"It's a joke, I suppose. Something like that."

"This wasn't the work of some toothless Utyl hesk smoker with a rusted needle. Who gave it to you?"

He finished a swirl, driving the chisel blade into the wood. Eris waited.

"Raisha," he muttered. "She was a linguist."

They sat a little longer, him carving vines and flowers and birds, her staring out at the flatlands. The sun hit the saltpan with blinding intensity, but the shadowline stayed black as ink.

"You should not cross to Mkalis again," said Eris.

"Didn't you promise to kill me?"

She said nothing.

"Will you still serve as my guide?"

She stood. "Remember to eat."

Vasethe continued to work on his table after Eris left, but his single-minded devotion to the task was gone. He set aside his tools. The rest of the project would wait. He dusted off his clothes and headed to the clean coolness of the kitchen.

Chapter Seven

ERIS'S BLOOD BURNED ON HIS TONGUE.

Vasethe opened his eyes to a vast yellow ocean. The waves moved in slow motion, water rising like treacle, reaching its full, shining height, then falling at the same languid pace. The beach was glass, incandescent and smooth, honeycombed by large circular funnels along the line of the tide. Above, a too-large sun gleamed through banks of cloud, reflecting off the surface of the water.

He turned to take in his surroundings. He stood at the border of the realm, on a sparse, arid slope. A few feet away, the hillside dissolved into a nothingness that was deeper and darker than blackness. The yawning emptiness made his head spin.

"I fixed your leg."

Eris sat at the base of a feather-leaved tree, her head resting against the trunk. Her Mkalis body was striking; more graceful and less human than her appearance in Ahri. Her skin had turned obsidian, flecked with emerald freckles across her arms and face, and her features confused the eye—too wide-set or too large. Glittering black hair framed her alien face with wild iridescence.

"Last time, I mended the bone before returning to Ahri. I've never been very good at curative magic, so that was about the extent of my abilities."

"Thank you."

She groaned and stood up.

"This is Buyak's realm?" asked Vasethe.

"A backwater corner of it. We'll need to head for the heartlands to obtain permissions from him. It's a long way to go."

"Are you okay?"

"I've been better." She gestured towards his neck. "That hex is a problem."

Vasethe touched his throat. Maggots floundered in the wet carnage. They had grown in number.

"It came into effect the moment you crossed the shadowline. I'm absorbing the effects on your behalf, but it means my own powers are, well, restrained."

Vasethe frowned, remembering the fiery agony he had experienced in the cottage. "And last time?"

"I slipped up once or twice."

"Is there a way of removing it?"

She smiled. "A few. Killing whoever laid it would work. Some demon rulers can get rid of hexes for a price, and your own death would erase it before you passed on to Mkalis."

"All of those options have significant drawbacks."

She smiled. "Don't worry; my pain tolerance far exceeds yours. I can handle it."

A skittering sound. They both looked towards the beach. Over the treacherous glass, a giant red-and-gold crab weaved from one passage to another.

"I owe you for this," Vasethe said.

"I look forward to a fully redecorated house." Eris laughed. "Come on."

She picked her way down the slope and Vasethe followed. The turf was bleached and dry and crunched underfoot. When he stepped onto the beach, the glass produced a hollow ringing sound, like distant bells. Through the haze of misted reflections he could see strange shapes, tunnels, vast caverns beneath him. Eris walked more lightly. Her reflection shifted and dissolved within the glass. Watching, Vasethe saw flashes of disparate figures, incongruent colours, sudden flickers of scarlet, the glimmer of steel. His own reflection remained steady, if unclear.

The crab registered their approach and halted. With difficulty, it lowered its front legs and tucked in its pincers into the semblance of a bow.

"Greetings, guests of his holiness Kan Buyak, God-King of the 200th realm of Mkalis, Lord of Fluttering Wings, Speaker of Absolutes," it said. Its voice was rasping but oddly childlike. "I am Lanesh, sanctified guide to those travelling the Hollow Way."

"Hello, Lanesh," said Eris. "I am the border keeper, here to escort this mortal through your god's realm."

"Hello," said Vasethe.

Lanesh bowed lower. "It is an honour."

The crab's ruby carapace possessed a translucent sheen. The shape of a small, twisted body lay frozen inside the creature, one hand raised as if to claw its way free of Lanesh's chitinous shell. Vasethe's eyes traced the irregular, buckled carapace—knees at a gross angle to the thighs, a hipbone warped and broken, the faint ridges of spasming toes—but he did not say anything.

"We wish to request an audience with Kan Buyak for the purpose of acquiring permission to enter another realm," said Eris.

Lanesh straightened, raised and lowered his pincers once. "The Solstice Assembly begins a week from today. His Radiance will be available to hear requests before the festivities commence."

"Ah, good. That's convenient."

Vasethe noticed the child's fingers twitch beneath the carapace, a tiny ripple of fractured bones. Eris's eyes flicked towards the movement, then away again.

"I am at your service," said Lanesh. "May we depart?"

"Yes, thank you."

The crab bobbed. "We will use the wistweed passage. I must warn you that straying from the path may lead to drowning. This way." He bowed again and scuttled backwards, zigzagging across the beach towards the entrance of a tunnel.

Vasethe leaned nearer to Eris. "Is there a child inside that crab?"

"The child *is* the crab," she replied. "A dweller who disobeyed a rule."

Vasethe stared at the fragile form inside the shell.

"Honoured guests!" Lanesh called, waving a pincer. "We should leave before the tide rises."

Eris gave Vasethe a warning glare and strode to the mouth of the tunnel. Unearthly whistling sounds issued from the passage as the slow water washed back and forth. The tunnel dropped downwards sharply; once inside, climbing out again would prove near impossible.

"Umbakur is some distance," said Lanesh. "We must move quickly to reach it before the passage floods."

Vasethe crouched beside the crab and laid his palm on the carapace above the child's grasping hand.

"Thank you for helping us," he said.

Lanesh scurried out of Vasethe's reach, pincers raised and clacking.

"It is my duty, as Guide of the Hollow Way." His tone was difficult to decipher, but he was clearly agitated. "I serve my ruler as best I am able."

"Sorry. I meant no offense."

Lanesh flexed his pincers once more, then lowered them. He scuttled back to the mouth of the tunnel, giving Vasethe a wide berth.

"This way, please." He slipped over the lip and slid down into the darkness.

"Lesson learnt?" Eris asked.

Vasethe sighed. He lowered himself down into the salt-scented tunnel after Lanesh.

The passage widened as they descended deeper beneath the ocean. The keening echoes of the waves emanated from all around; the noise grew louder and quieter but never fell entirely silent. At times, the wailing sounded human.

Lanesh's claws clicked against the ground. Like the sound of Eris's wards in Ahri. Vasethe glanced at her. She raised an eyebrow and he looked away. The hex did not seem to be affecting her too severely.

The passage levelled out. Above, swift fish cut through the ocean depths, and wispy lights gleamed in the distance. Obscured by bends in the tunnel, it was difficult to determine their source, but to Vasethe's eyes the lights appeared to move. He squinted. Too far; he could not make them out.

"What is Umbakur?" he asked Lanesh.

The crab's stalked eyes swivelled, focussed on him.

"The midpoint. It does not flood when the water comes," he said.

"Is it an island?"

Lanesh waved his pincers as he walked.

"Mkalis geography is flexible," said Eris, "and our guide does not want to lie."

Vasethe paused. "Is lying accidentally . . ."

"Still an untruth."

"I'll watch my words, then."

"Ah, but I think you always do." Her teeth flashed. "Don't you?"

He smiled, said nothing.

The tunnel branched, one side clear and empty, the other tangled with bone-white kelp. The kelp reeked of dying things and Lanesh veered to avoid it. The child inside his shell was still now.

When Vasethe had touched him, the broken fingers had moved.

One of the lights drew nearer. It bobbed in the water outside, bright and curious. As Vasethe and Eris passed, it shot forward and latched onto the glass with rows of needled suckers. Lanesh jumped.

"I have never seen them do that before," he said.

Somewhere between a squid and a jellyfish, the creature was no larger than a clenched fist. It glowed with sickly blue luminance in the dark water. As they stepped forward, it detached from the glass.

"What is it?" Vasethe asked.

It drifted along the outside of the tunnel, keeping pace with them.

"Persistent." Eris eyed it.

"I call them lightfish," said Lanesh. "It is probably just confused. They are usually shy creatures."

The lightfish smashed into the glass again.

Lanesh, for all his reassurances, kept close watch on the creature. He did not comment when two more drifted in from the gloom. The creatures appeared oblivious to one another, colliding as they crashed against the tunnel wall.

Vasethe stopped.

"Hold on for a moment," he said.

"Honoured guest, I do not think that is wise; we must reach Umbakur."

Vasethe walked a few paces back and stopped again. The lightfish paused in their assault.

"Arrogant, wouldn't you say?" Eris frowned as one of the creatures swam towards Vasethe, then changed direction and returned to its position directly above her. "But interesting."

The creatures resumed their assault. She did not flinch.

"Well, I thought that the hex might be the cause of their—" Vasethe broke off.

"What?"

He turned and gazed down the shadowy passage behind them.

The tunnel was empty, but the smell of lilies and ash lingered in the air. Faint, barely perceptible.

"Never mind," he said.

The passage branched once more. Lanesh kept left, moving a little quicker than before. Vasethe glanced over his shoulder and shivered.

They found the body dredged up at the next intersection. He lay face-down, legs entangled with hollow tubes of brittle coral. His feet had been severed and replaced by meat hooks, metal soldered to bones and bloody flesh, and his shock of silky black hair was still damp. It obscured his face. The skin of his hands had worn raw; one arm stretched forward as if to grasp Vasethe's ankle. He must have dragged himself through the tunnels, only to be caught by the tide. Eris barely looked at the corpse.

"Don't touch him," she warned. "He's not dead."

Vasethe's eyes widened. "Shouldn't we help him, then?"

"No."

"Eris, come on."

She sighed and rolled up her sleeves.

"Honoured border keeper, I really would not recommend—"

She strode forward, grabbed a fistful of the man's hair, and yanked him upright.

The man had no face—only a toothless, slavering mouth that stretched from hairline to jaw. As Eris pulled his head back, he produced a wet gurgling sound, then screamed.

The noise brought Vasethe to his knees. He grasped his head in his hands, and Lanesh cowered behind him. The scream rose in pitch, unearthly and awful, yet Vasethe could hear whispering beneath it; a voice spoke right into his ear.

"Come closer, come closer, let me, closer, let me closer, come, let me, skin, let me, eat, closer, let me hold . . ."

The man's terrible legs lashed out, but Eris evaded them. She grasped his jaw with her free hand and wrenched sideways. His neck snapped. The screaming stopped.

"Closer . . ."

The echoes faded down the tunnel and the thumping of the lightfish grew louder. Vasethe leaned against the wall, catching his breath.

"I warned you," said Eris, quite calmly, "that Mkalis is dangerous. This is not Ahri. You will listen to me, or you will die."

There was a new, hoarse edge to her voice. She cleared her throat and winced.

"This way," Lanesh whispered.

They walked. The lightfish hit the glass. Intersection after intersection, but now the way forward had become less clear. The kelp thickened across the tunnel floor, spreading waxy feelers over their path. It gave underfoot like skin, pliant and smooth, and its sharp smell made it difficult for Vasethe to think straight.

They came across more bodies concealed by the kelp, only their bloated limbs poking out. The corpses were human in shape but mutilated. Most were missing feet, some arms, and crude hooks and barbs protruded from their swollen, leaking wounds. All the bodies lay face-down.

Drip.

The pounding of the lightfish formed one indistinguishable wall of sound. The shoal was everywhere, blinding and packed tight, the water obscured by their bodies. Through the noise, the dripping should have been inaudible.

Drip.

A single dart of pain shot through Vasethe's throat. The kelp under his feet was wet. Eris brushed a drop of water from her cheek.

"Here, come closer, here . . ."

He swayed. Eris reached out and steadied him. The voice was different, a woman this time. She was washed up against the wall a few feet away. A reel of barbed wire punctured the skin of her stomach and thighs, leaving pinpricks of black. His vision swam. Eris dug her fingernails into his arm, and the whispering quieted.

The glass made an eerie groaning sound punctuated by brief pops. As Vasethe watched, fractures branched through the roof in lightning streaks. Spray jetted from the cracks.

Could she breathe underwater? he wondered.

"There is the terminus." Lanesh sped over the ground, his claws finding purchase between the slick kelp.

They rounded a bend in the passage. Ahead, the tunnel ended. Vasethe blinked. The ocean just stopped, like someone had cut a funnel through the water. In the centre of this impossible abyss hovered a colossal granite mass. Umbakur. A web of slender bridges connected the fortress to the tunnels; it sat like a fat spider between them. All around, the unnatural waters dropped slowly into the bowls of the earth, silent as blood seeping into fabric.

A crunching, splintering sound was all the warning they received. Eris yanked Vasethe onto the bridge just as the tunnel cracked, and a torrent of razor-edged glass thundered down behind them. A shard sliced into the back of Vasethe's calf. Lanesh, only a few feet ahead of them, was almost pushed off the bridge as the water gushed over him. Eris's hand shot up and the crab froze, teetering on the edge. She drew him back to safer ground.

Water poured over the edges of the bridge, but they were out of its reach. Eris nudged a flopping lightfish with her foot, sending it tumbling into the darkness below. Vasethe's vision steadied. He could breathe more easily here.

Behind them the water slowed, like it was thickening, coagulating, and closed the entrance to the wistweed passage.

Chapter Eight

NO ONE GUARDED the rusted gates. The air whistled around the edifice and was sent swirling into the abyss. Up close, Umbakur looked larger still. Windowless, blunt, hewn from stone, and dropped into the sea. A shiver ran down Vasethe's spine. Lanesh placed his claws into twin holes bored through the surface of the bridge, and the doors swung open.

"Welcome to Umbakur," he said.

As they crossed the threshold into the fortress, the interior brightened. Flames sprang to life along the length of the narrow hall.

With a juddering whine, the gates shut behind them. The air smelled of sweat and fear. Strings of yellow paper lanterns hung from the damp-mottled ceiling, each scrawled with words in old alphabets. Vasethe's brow furrowed. Woven tapestries covered the walls, dampening sound, but he could still hear screaming. Intermittent, distant, emanating from deeper within.

"The guest quarters are this way. Once the tides change, we will be able to continue," Lanesh said.

"Thank you for your help," said Eris.

Lanesh waved his pincers. "It was gracious of you to save me on the bridge," he replied, "although next time, I would ask for you not to."

"Noted."

"Please excuse me; I am expected by the Census Taker. If you head to the right, you should find your rooms."

Eris turned to Vasethe, who was staring at the lanterns. "Come on, you're bleeding on Buyak's nice, clean floor."

He glanced down and saw that the gash in his calf still weeping. From far above them, he heard a shriek.

Eris raised the corner of a tapestry to reveal a slender, high-peaked archway. She stepped through and motioned for him to follow. "I should to return to Ahri. Just for a few hours, to recuperate and check on the shadow-line."

"Will our vessels be safe here?"

She pursed her lips. "It would be an incredible breach of etiquette for Buyak to allow harm to befall an acknowledged guest. Let alone me."

"And yet, the lightfish."

The guestroom was warm and low-roofed and contained six narrow pallets. A mural covered the wall behind the beds: a silver-eyed god in a robe of purple feathers, his hands cupping his ears. Egrets surrounded him, their wings spread like fans and their slim necks bent in deference. The tips of their feathers were leafed in gold.

"Ordinarily, I would have concealed my body in the borders between realms." She frowned. "But I am not sure your vessel could withstand that. Besides, we would need to find a channel to cross."

"I could wait here."

"Stand guard, you mean." She gestured to a pallet. He sat. "The longer you remain in Mkalis, the more the bonds to your true body will fray. Stay long enough, and the surrogate vessel will start to leave hooks in your soul. They will drag you back here, and you will unravel." She rolled up the leg of his pants to look at the injury. "Your conscience will fade, but it won't be death in the real sense. So, what's left of you will permanently linger in this realm, never to be reborn. A ghost."

Eris spat into her hand and pressed her palm to the cut. Her eyes flashed red, and Vasethe's leg jerked.

"We have only been in Mkalis for a few hours," he said. The cut burned, then itched. He tried to keep a neutral expression. "Would the hex revert to me in your absence?"

She raised her gaze and looked him straight in the eyes. "I can stop it from reverting. So, if you want to stay, then stay. It's your decision."

Her eyes were so black that they seemed to absorb

light. Vasethe experienced a strange kind of pull this close to her, like he might be falling forward , like currents were dragging him from the shore.

"I'll stay," he said.

Eris nodded. "I won't be too long, but call out my name if anything happens. I will come."

She straightened. Vasethe breathed out softly, still off-balance. A memory—the shadow of a memory—troubled his mind. Something important. Something lost. It slipped away.

Eris took the pallet furthest from the archway. She lay on her back and closed her eyes. A strange stillness settled over her, and after a while, her chest ceased to move.

Vasethe flexed his calf. No pain; only a thin white scar to mark the injury. He stood, tested his weight on the leg.

"Sorry," he murmured to Eris.

The corridor outside was deserted. Vasethe moved soundlessly, inspecting the lanterns. The cuneiform symbols were smudged and untidy but had similarities to Linish letters.

Each lantern bore a different message. Vasethe thought they might be confessions. Strange confessions, admissions of mispronouncing a certain name, of having grey eyes. Vasethe's knowledge of the language was too limited for full understanding, but again and again, the word for "forge."

The tang of molten metal burned in his mouth.

He reached a stairwell, paused, then headed up. The tapestries here were woven from darker threads, earthy browns and deep greens stitched into stiff geometric patterns.

Ahead, he could hear voices.

"—anything of that nature before. We must assume the creatures reacted for a reason." A purring, genderless voice. "My lord is no doubt aware."

"No doubt." A female voice. "I imagine the keeper is displeased. This probably wasn't the reception she anticipated."

They drew closer. Vasethe lifted the edge of a tapestry and ducked inside the archway behind it.

"I believe His Radiance will make the appropriate apologies."

"I think that will depend on the circumstances of their reunion. Buyak's spine is flexible, but only up to a point."

"I wasn't suggesting he would bow and scrape, Your Grace."

The couple passed the tapestry. Vasethe held his breath.

"He will do as the situation demands. If he can avoid a premature altercation with her, I believe he will. Similarly, if he can feign innocence, or at least ignorance, he will."

"Wise is the Lord of Fluttering Wings."

"That is subjective." Their voices grew softer as they walked down the stairs. "'Shrewd,' I would say, is more accurate."

Vasethe exhaled slowly and edged out from behind the tapestry. The corridor was empty once more. He glanced towards the stairs, then shook his head and carried on.

The sounds of movement and activity increased as he moved deeper into the fortress. There were fewer wall hangings here, and the décor was more utilitarian. Bare black walls gleamed, hard crystal catching the lantern light. Through the archways, he could see a series of similar rooms, all unoccupied. The same mural on the walls, the same egrets and the same metal-eyed god. Buyak himself, presumably. Sticks of incense rested in glass bowls at the god's feet; their smoke curled lazily upwards.

Vasethe came to a junction and turned left into a smaller passageway. Someone—or something—was moaning; he followed the sound. It struck him as strange that none of the rooms had doors.

The sounds of pain came from within the next room. He slowed to a halt outside the archway and pressed his back to the wall. Steeling himself, he peered around the entrance.

The creature lay curled in the corner, its eyes fixed on

the ground. Limbs were missing and mangled and out of place, and low, persistent moans emerged from the bloody remains of its jaw. With every whimper, Vasethe could see the raw fluttering of its exposed larynx.

It did not react to him. Even if it was capable of movement, it could never have posed a threat. Too broken. The emptiness of its eyes transfixed Vasethe. Blank, like the gaze of a doll.

The creature moaned more loudly and Vasethe. He stepped through the archway. Buyak's eyes bored into him from the mural.

The creature did not so much as twitch when Vasethe knelt beside it. Ribbons of skin swathed its spine, the glint of vertebrae visible through the gore. Which rule had it broken? Vasethe gazed up at Buyak. Had it lied? Had it used the wrong honorific, wandered somewhere forbidden? The god remained silent.

Vasethe reached out and touched the creature's head. No response. Whatever sentience it had possessed was gone. He cupped the base of its head, supported the weight of its skull as warm blood oozed over his fingers. With steady hands, Vasethe twisted to the right.

The bones gave as easily as a bird's. One sharp snap. The creature stopped moaning. Vasethe laid it down and gently closed its wide, empty eyes. In death, its body seemed to shrink.

"I hope you will find a better life in Ahri," he murmured.

The lantern at the door flared with a *whoosh,* then ebbed and extinguished. Vasethe glanced up but could see no one there. The lantern swung back and forth, touched by a breeze.

He wiped his hands on the floor and stood. Time to return to Eris.

He retraced his steps, back down the corridor and then the broader passage, then stopped.

The stairs were gone.

He ran his fingertips over the smooth surface of the wall. Ancient, impenetrable. Cold. Vasethe paused for a moment, then turned and retreated down the passage.

Mkalis geography is flexible.

From every cell, Buyak watched him. When new sounds of moaning commenced, Vasethe did not investigate their source. The scent of creosote and ash drifted through the air. It grew stronger.

A different set of stairs, leading downwards. A draft ran icy fingers through his hair. He descended.

The next corridor was darker; there were no lanterns, and only the thin light from the floor above illuminated Vasethe's way. The walls were black mirrors, casting a cascade of thousands of reflections of his vessel. It was the first time he had seen his surrogate body's face, and he paused, struck by the strangeness of his eyes. In shape, not unusual, perhaps larger than his real ones, the skin around them smoother. But his irises were uncanny; a ring of blood red, swirling like clouds.

He shook his head and advanced down the passage.

Over here...

The voice in his head was soft. It passed like a stray thought, something quickly forgotten. He almost failed to notice it, but the whispering persisted.

This way.

Vasethe stiffened as he perceived the tugging sensation around his chest. He took a step backwards and a wave of dizziness caused him to stumble.

"Dammit," he muttered. His thoughts moved as if through thick sand, and he reached out to stabilise himself against the wall.

His hand met another.

Vasethe's head jerked up and he locked eyes with his reflection. Red eyes, burning. Hungry. Slowly, slowly, a smile spread across his reflection's face. Its grip tightened.

Recovering from his shock, Vasethe tried to wrench his arm free.

"Eri—" The name did not escape his lips.

The world went black and wind roared in his ears like a hurricane. Someone was laughing and the sound shook him to his core. A thick and viscous substance lurched and pressed beneath his skin, the sensation abhorrent, leeches squirming through his flesh. He could not see, could not move, could not make a sound.

Confess.

The voice was like those of the faceless monsters in the wistweed passage, and this time, Eris could not save him. The smell of molten metal overwhelmed him.

The forge.

The knowledge came to him from nowhere, but he *knew* that his soul would be consumed, not a death but an unholy, endless bleeding into the most forbidden, debased, *vile* . . .

"It's not your time."

Vasethe's lungs flooded with air. He clutched his throat. The rushing in his ears stopped, the crawling of his skin stilled. He retched and opened his eyes.

"Are you hurt?"

He was back in the guest quarters, lying on a pallet. A woman stood above him.

Without meaning to, Vasethe glanced towards Eris.

The woman followed his eyes. "Don't worry; she's still sleeping," she said. "But not for much longer, I'd imagine. The tides are changing."

With shaking arms, Vasethe raised himself into a sitting position. "Did you save me?"

"I brought you back here. You should be more careful,

wandering around on your own. Especially with your guardian indisposed."

The woman was milk-skinned and green-eyed. Waves of bone-white hair flowed over her bare breasts, down to her waist. She wore a shimmering skirt that pooled on the ground at her feet. Something about her reminded Vasethe of Eris.

"Thank you," he said.

She did not acknowledge him but turned, and suddenly she stood beside Eris. Vasethe had not seen her take a single step. She leaned over the border keeper, studying her face.

Vasethe struggled to his feet. "Have we met before?"

"How could that be, Ahri-dweller?" she said distractedly. Her hair brushed Eris's cheek.

"I'm not sure. But your face seems familiar."

The woman looked at Vasethe in amusement. "Perhaps in another life." She ran a finger along the length of Eris's jaw; a gentle, almost affectionate gesture. Her nails were long, green.

"Don't—" He took a few steps and his knees buckled. Cool hands propped him upright before he could fall. The woman was taller. He flinched.

"Careful," she said.

"Who are you?"

"Maybe next time. Look after her for me, won't you?"

She vanished and Vasethe crumpled to the ground. His knees hit stone with a painful thud, and he swore. For some reason, his hands were shaking.

He picked himself up and sat on the edge of a pallet.

"Eris."

She stirred. Her eyes opened.

"Feeling better?"

"I never told you I felt unwell." She sat and pushed her hair back from her face. "What's wrong?"

"The tides are changing, so we should probably be ready to move."

Her dark eyes lingered on his face. "Onwards, then."

Chapter Nine

LANESH RETURNED MOMENTS LATER. Vasethe tried to conceal his unsteadiness, leaning against the wall. The crab performed a quick bow.

"I hope that your rest was comfortable," he said. "Given the collapse of the wistweed passage, I think it would be best for us to take a different route to the mainland. I would like to avoid the risk of further complications."

"What did you have in mind?" asked Eris.

"My lord maintains a friendship with Res Tiba, ruler of the 713th realm, Sower of Bones. I have acquired the relevant permissions via the Census Taker, who is at liberty to grant access to travellers deemed important to Kan Buyak."

"Buyak is friends with a demon?" Vasethe asked.

"Careful, stranger; your knowledge is showing," said Eris.

"Res Tiba is said to be worthy of my lord's benefaction," Lanesh said, a little stiffly.

"Given what I know of Tiba, Buyak should be glad that

they're on good terms." Eris seemed amused. "Crossing through her realm will take us to the mainland?"

"Yes, border keeper."

"Let's do it, then. Would you tell us the pertinent rules?"

Lanesh bobbed once and recited without pause: "A duel cannot be refused. A duel must end in death. Do not speak to inhabitants of the 713th realm, unless to initiate a duel. Do not move in the presence of Res Tiba unless granted permission."

"Thank you, Lanesh," Eris said.

Lanesh bobbed again. "This way." He scuttled out through the archway.

Eris eyed Vasethe as he straightened. "What's bothering you?"

"Well, I seem to have been hexed, and I'm not sure I deserved it, and those lightfish were unpleasant."

"You know that isn't what I meant."

"It's probably best to discuss it in Ahri."

Eris hesitated and followed his gaze to the mural of Buyak. She nodded.

Lanesh moved through Umbakur with surety. The dark-walled fortress was quieter now; the screaming had stopped. They rounded a corner and came to a new set of gates. A breeze flowed through the gaps between the metal bars. The sky outside was a rich black, starless and secret.

"You have blood on your hands again," Eris said, without looking at Vasethe.

"Not mine." The sound of the creature's pitiful moaning resounded in his mind.

She did not press the issue.

They crossed another bridge to a tunnel both wider and higher than the wistweed passage. Although it was difficult to make out details in the dark, the water surrounding the tunnel seemed to possess a teal shimmer.

"It is not too far," Lanesh said.

A cold wind blew towards them, carrying the smell of wet soil and bluegum sap. Vasethe could hear the rustling of leaves, rising and fading like ripples. The blue sheen grew brighter as they walked.

"Do you take travellers this way often?" Eris asked Lanesh.

"Only once before, border keeper. On most occasions, it would be the Census Taker who accompanies guests through Res Tiba's realm." He paused. "I requested to continue as your guide."

"I'm glad," said Eris.

Vasethe looked backwards. Deep darkness obscured the tunnel behind them, Buyak's realm fading.

The light ahead resolved into shapes and colours. They stepped from the tunnel into the shadow of tall trees. Fine specks of rain misted the air, swirling in gentle spirals as the breeze shifted. The chirrups of unseen birds filtered down from the canopy above, somewhere nearby a stream gurgled. The loose earth was soft under Vasethe's heels.

Lanesh turned and gestured down the slope. "The channel back to Buyak's realm is through the Bone Grove."

Eris gazed upwards at the swaying dark green leaves. Water collected on her hair and lashes, and her expression was difficult to interpret, distracted and perhaps sad.

"Eris?" Vasethe ventured.

She lowered her gaze and smiled. The expression did not reach her eyes.

"Just enjoying the rain," she said. "Lead on."

The low sounds of the forest accompanied them through the trees. The undergrowth was sparse—only lichen-covered boulders and fallen branches impeded their passage. Mushrooms sprang up from the shadows; the pale-barked trees groaned a little in the wind. Tiny lilac birds darted above their heads.

The slope levelled and the trees thinned to reveal a gleaming expanse of water. The lake shone pearl grey beneath the dense bank of clouds. Small waves lapped along the shore and a rowboat swayed in the water. As they approached, Vasethe realized the vessel was lined with shell, the interior streaked with crests of iridescence.

Eris stumbled and he reached out to steady her. She cursed under her breath and glared at him.

"It's slippery," he said.

She pulled her arm out of his grasp.

"The hex still hurts you, doesn't it? Returning to Ahri didn't help."

"It's fine." She stepped into the boat and settled down on the rear bench. "Make yourself useful and row."

Lanesh clambered aboard and crouched in the middle of the boat, pressing his pincers and legs close to his carapace. Leaning over him, Vasethe saw that the child inside his shell had relaxed somewhat and curled into a foetal position.

He pushed the vessel a little deeper into the water and jumped in, causing the craft to rock dangerously.

"If you upturn this boat . . ." Eris fixed him with an evil look.

"A curse for the next twenty lives?"

"That would be lenient of me."

The oars were light and smooth in his hands. Vasethe stretched and curled his fingers around the handles, then dipped the paddles into the water and pulled. They glided forward onto the lake. Eris leaned back and closed her eyes, her lips parted to catch the rain.

Vasethe rowed evenly. The water scattered light as he cut through the surface, and shoals of pale blue and silver fish swam in their wake. A flock of waterfowl watched them from the shallows before melting into the reeds, and a lone kite hovered far above, her wingtips fluttering in the cool breeze.

"A region of his realm was like this," Eris said quietly, her eyes still shut. "Yett, I mean. Rivers and lakes and trees. He made it rain the first time I met him."

Vasethe took a while before answering. "That sounds discourteous."

"Maybe. He was like that. He had just ascended. I think he meant it as a kind of joke, or maybe he was testing me. But I liked it. It was . . . different." She lapsed into silence for a while. "Shade and cool water have always seemed like gifts to me."

"Comes with living in a desert."

"Hm. I know." She opened her eyes. "But a desert makes you hard and sharp and dangerous, and all this"—she gestured to encompass the landscape around her—"just makes your thoughts hazy. Makes you soft."

Rain dripped from Vasethe's chin. He brushed it away. "You disagree?"

"No." He shook his head. "No, I don't. But I was thinking that your job asks too much of you."

"Job?" She weighed the word. "I don't really consider being the border keeper a job. I'm not like you, jumping from one occupation to the next. My 'job' is somewhere between what I am and what I live for."

"Except during his life."

She opened her mouth to argue, then closed it again.

"Is that where we're supposed to go, Lanesh?" Vasethe turned and pointed past Eris's shoulder.

The lake narrowed into a channel surrounded by rustling trees. Thirteen enormous towers arose from both sides of the forest edge, yellow and pitted and curved inwards to almost touch at their summits. Looping swing bridges ran between them. Vasethe could just make out strange figures crossing them.

"Yes, that is our destination," said Lanesh. "The Bone Grove was built from the ribcage of the 713th realm's former ruler. Res Tiba resides within."

Vasethe rested the oars above the water and allowed the current to guide their boat into the channel. Beneath the ribs, the trees had been cleared to make room for thatch-roofed buildings. Ivory sculptures rested on raised buoys, painted birds and fish scaled with smooth river pebbles. Streams ran between the buildings, and a number of small boats bobbed on the lazy waves.

Vasethe started and snatched up the oars when their vessel lurched sideways. A leaf-green reptile streaked by, webbed human hands powering through the water. Beneath the surface, colossal honeycomb structures supported the bulk of the bone towers, providing homes to the denizens of the lake. He caught glints of bright scales and smooth hides through the murk.

The shadow of a rib darkened the water. At Lanesh's instruction, Vasethe manoeuvred the craft to a small dock and climbed out. The slick wooden deck was covered in yellow algae. He offered Eris a hand. She looked at it, then reached out and clasped his wrist.

"I've decided to make a stop before returning to Buyak's realm," she said.

Lanesh hopped over the gunwale. He hooked one pincer over the side of the dock and pulled himself up.

"As you wish," he said. "Where would you like to go?"

"Can you take me to Tiba?"

A pause.

"I—I can request an audience with the relevant authorities—"

"That won't be necessary. I just need to know where she is."

"Border keeper, with respect, such a breach of etiquette is not recommended."

Eris grinned. "Oh, Mkalis has forgotten how I operate, hasn't it? Don't worry, Lanesh; I only want to make a request."

Lanesh stepped from side to side, anxious.

"It won't take long."

"Yes, border keeper. Of course." He sighed and hurried down the jetty.

Vasethe looped a length of rope around the cleat on the dock, securing the rowboat. "What are you up to?"

She leaned closer and spoke so that only he could hear.

"Buyak knew about the lightfish. As Tiba is his ally, I'd like to ask her some questions."

"Ask, or . . ."

"I doubt she'll be cooperative, so I may need to draw on more of my power."

"The hex will revert to me?"

"If there is a confrontation, yes, but I hope it won't come to that."

"It's fine."

She nodded. "It would be a short fight, anyway. Outside of the fifty highest realms, no ruler presents much of a threat to me."

He smiled. "Scary."

"I am, aren't I? Come, our guide is miserable enough as is; let's not keep him waiting."

The ribs divided the settlement into bands of brightness and shadow; rays of sunlight scattered silver across the lake. The smell of damp thatch and river weed was thick in the air. The wooden walkways creaked under their weight, but otherwise the village was quiet.

Then the world twisted and Vasethe found himself

hundreds of feet above the ground. The lake spun in his vision.

Stay calm.

Eris's voice resounded inside his mind.

"I believe that you wanted to talk to me?" said someone behind him.

Vasethe could not move, could not even blink. Eris had paralysed him to ensure that he adhered to the realm's rules. He knelt on a transparent platform suspended between the peaks of the ribs.

"It was kind of you to pick us up. I was dreading the stairs." Eris's voice had a different resonance now, louder, like she might be speaking to more than one person. His throat twinged. *"Allow me to move, and we can have a civil conversation."*

"It has been, what, four hundred years? And yet here you are, the same as ever. Or perhaps ... reduced." Tiba had a strange voice, multiple people speaking in perfect unison. Her feet appeared within Vasethe's line of vision: four of them, three-toed, taloned, the colour of river mud. She wore anklets of fingerbones. They clinked together when she walked. "After all this time, still pining after your dead god."

A flock of birds passed below them, black arrows shooting south.

"Grant me permission to move, demon."

"I want you to leave my realm now. Whatever you came for, I have no interest in helping you."

Vasethe's throat burned.

"You misunderstand me. That was not a request. Grant me permission to move, or I will kill you. Slowly. And when I am done, I will be the ruler of your pitiful realm and all your subjects."

"You're making threats?" Tiba began to laugh, an awful seesawing sound.

Vasethe's body jerked forward, as if a rope around his waist had been wrenched by a giant hand. His feet barely touched the ground. He hurtled forward and, in the same movement, his hand snatched a dagger from the demon's belt and drove it into her collar.

Tiba stopped laughing. Vasethe's hand pulled out the blade with a wet sucking sound. She coughed. Blood flecked the platform, drops splattering Vasethe's face.

"Last warning."

"H-how?" the demon hissed. The wound gushed black blood.

"'Do not move in the presence of Res Tiba unless granted permission.' There was nothing to stop me from moving someone else. Did you really think that your little restriction could stop me? Give up, Tiba."

"I won't let you touch my dwellers."

"I only want to talk. But don't test me."

Tiba coughed again. "You have permission to move."

The pain in Vasethe's throat decreased. He took a shuddering breath and backed away from the demon, looking at her properly for the first time.

Tiba was twice Eris's size. Her skintight sheath was ripped and soaked in oily black blood. Thick braids brushed her calves, hanging like ropes down her back. She had spread her wings, both the length of Vasethe's body, and scarlet tattoos covered their surface. She glared at Eris. Each of her pupils split into two half-moons.

Eris placed a hand on Vasethe's shoulder, steadying him. *"Change the rule so that I can speak aloud without the need for a duel."*

"You should have stayed out of Mkalis," Tiba spat.

"Cooperate, and you will have nothing to fear from me."

"What do you want?"

"I will not ask again."

Tiba growled. She touched the wound with her fingers and smeared the blood over her lips. Her legs trembled slightly.

"Guests may speak to the ruler of the realm without restraint," she said stiffly, her mouth stained glossy black.

The world rippled.

"Thank you." Eris inclined her head. "Please attend to your injury."

For a moment, Vasethe thought that the demon might

refuse purely to spite Eris. Then she touched blood to her lips a second time.

"Heal," she murmured, eyes downcast. She swayed and her wings folded. The seeping wound began to shrink, and Tiba's breathing eased.

"Let's start again," said Eris. "I greet you, Res Tiba, Sower of Bones, Ruler of the 713th Realm of Mkalis."

"Don't bother with decorum," Tiba said bitterly. "Whatever you want, just spit it out."

Eris scrutinised her for a moment.

"Information," she said.

Tiba eyed Vasethe, then swung her gaze back to Eris, wary as a snake. "Regarding?"

"Buyak."

"Oh." Some of the anger drained from Tiba's expression. She licked her lips clean. "That's all?"

"We'll see. Have you noticed any changes in his behaviour?"

"To be honest, we've never been close. I am not influential enough for that."

Eris looked down pointedly at the houses nestled at the base of the ribs.

"Yes, I think his recent behaviour has been strange."

"You think?"

"I'll tell you what I know, but why do you want the information?"

Eris considered before replying. "Creatures of his realm accosted me. I need to know if this was deliberate provocation."

"You mean, if he urged them to attack you?"

"Exactly."

Tiba mulled it over.

"He has never been reckless, so that would be out of character."

"But?"

"He's . . . he's changed. He's more confident, and perhaps with your current reputation, he might have thought—"

"What do the rulers of Mkalis say about me these days?" Eris asked.

Tiba was silent.

She sighed. "Never mind. Any idea why he might be feeling particularly bold?"

"There are whispers." A muscle in Tiba's jaw tensed. She lowered her voice.

"Over the last two hundred years, six realms have become untethered: 953, 921, 845, 914, 899, and then, just recently, 406."

"Res Kstille's realm." Eris frowned. "He's dead?"

"No one in the lower realms knows anything. Access to his domain just ceased, the channels vanished. He may have been assassinated, but he was tough and careful, one of the old guard. It wouldn't have been easy."

Eris looked disturbed. "And no new rulers have stepped forward to claim the realms?"

"They might have, but there hasn't been any kind of formal declaration. No one knows where the realms are now. It's as if they were annexed, then abandoned."

"That's not good," muttered Eris. "That really isn't good."

"Do you know something?" Tiba asked.

"I have suspicions. And, unfortunately, I think I've been trying to reach one of the untethered realms." She rubbed her forehead. "This is more complicated than I anticipated. Why do you suspect Buyak?"

"At the last assembly before his disappearance, Kstille got into a violent disagreement with Buyak. I wasn't there, but I heard that Kstille proposed a Tribunal of the High for Buyak's impeachment."

Eris whistled.

"Can you impeach a god?" asked Vasethe.

Both Tiba and Eris turned to look at him. Their gazes were equally disconcerting.

"Theoretically, yes," said Eris. "In all the years I've been border keeper, there have been three Tribunals. Only one succeeded. The grounds for a meeting of the High involve a ruler breaking the most fundamental laws of creation. If Kstille dared to suggest that Buyak could be struck from his throne, he must have discovered something damning."

"And with the disappearing realms and rulers . . ." Tiba shrugged.

"I catch your drift. And it would suggest the cause of his newfound arrogance." Eris scowled. "What a mess."

"It's all rumour, you understand."

"Of course. But I wouldn't put it past Buyak." She shook her head, clearing her thoughts. "In that case, I have one more request."

The demon nodded warily.

"The hex on this man's throat? Remove it."

Tiba's lips thinned. Eris raised her eyebrow fractionally and waited. Her stillness radiated danger, like a knife held to Tiba's windpipe. The wind whistled across the platform.

The demon nodded, the barest movement of her head. "I will try."

She beckoned to Vasethe. He stepped forward. With surprising gentleness, Tiba tilted his head upwards to examine the wound. Up close, she smelled of smoke and honey. He felt her breath on his skin and repressed a shiver.

"You are absorbing its malice?" she asked Eris.

"I am."

"Perhaps I underestimated you."

"You don't say."

Tiba inhaled deeply and frowned. "It's a strange hex. I don't know if interfering with it is a good idea; it might just kill him outright if I try to unstitch it."

"Then you'd better be careful."

"What do *you* want?" Tiba spoke to Vasethe directly for the first time. Her voice was kinder, and she looked him in the eyes. He held her gaze.

"Please do what you can," he said.

A rumbling noise rose from deep within her chest. Vasethe's throat stung and the maggots quivered. Tiba's frown deepened. "Who laid this?"

"Someone in Ahri," said Eris. "The hex has been present from the moment he crossed into Mkalis."

"Then why does it smell of the High?"

A pause. Eris shook her head. "That's impossible. I haven't let a ruler cross the shadowline in centuries."

Tiba sniffed again. "I'm certain of it. This is god-touched."

Eris pursed her lips. "Can you sense anything else?"

Tiba was quiet for a few seconds. Vasethe held his breath.

"Smells broken? Fragmented? Twisted somehow. The residue of the caster's magic is so faint that I can hardly detect it. It's . . ." She grimaced. "I don't know. It's difficult to put into words."

"Try."

Tiba hesitated. "It's waiting."

The wind chilled the sweat along Vasethe's spine. The maggots burrowed deeper into his flesh.

"I will let the malice revert just before you begin unstitching the hex," Eris said. She hesitated, before adding, "Be quick."

Tiba nodded.

"Ready?" she asked Vasethe.

He took a deep breath. "Yes."

The demon opened her jaws wide and bit into his throat. The world dissolved in white agony.

Chapter Ten

IT TOOK VASETHE a while to remember himself.

Eris poured tea down his throat until he choked. But even though he was securely back inside his Ahri body, he could not recognise himself, or her, could not remember how he had arrived in the unfamiliar bed at the edge of the desert, could not recall his family, where he grew up, what he had done, who he had loved, desire, language, faces, anything. A vision replayed in his mind, of standing beneath a waterfall in autumn, the rush of water against his skin, a voice drifting from trees. Later, he realised that the painting on Eris's wall matched the scene in his mind.

Eris coaxed him to eat. She seldom spoke, and her body was tight with anger. Although he could not understand her, she frightened him. He tried not to flinch when she moved.

Memories returned to him, arriving in sudden flashes of illumination. He lay awake in Eris's bed and waited for all the pieces to accumulate and fit together. Night fell. The low growling, crunching sound of the Ageless pressed against the window panes. When they left, all was quiet. The moonlight had gathered in a quicksilver river in the doorway.

Vasethe rose.

Eris stood in the yard. She did not say anything when Vasethe passed, but her eyes tracked him as he staggered from the front door to the fence. His fingers struggled with the latch on the gate; the hinges protested, and it swung open.

Salt glittered like rain against the sand; the coarse crystals bit into the soles of his bare feet. He walked past the train tracks, away from the house and the shadowline and everything else. His breathing was laboured; his blunt fingernails dug crescents into his scar on his neck.

Although the sand was level and smooth, Vasethe stumbled. His legs folded and he fell to his knees. Every loss he had ever suffered cut into him like glass, every cruelty and mistake, every failure. He began to get up, then stopped and sank back to the ground.

Eris disappeared into her house, leaving the gate unlatched.

In the morning, Vasethe was back beside the table in the yard, carving. The sounds of chipping and scratching began just before sunrise. When Eris emerged, he appeared calm. He worked with his usual methodical precision.

Eris set a teacup within his reach. Her shift was torn

The Border Keeper

and a welt was visible across her right shoulder.

"A long night," she said.

Vasethe smiled. His expression was all wrong; too bright, lips stretched too far. Eris studied him, her own face blank. Tiba had not cured him; the demon's efforts had warped something inside him, or perhaps brought an old injury nearer to the surface.

"Do you have all your memories back?" she asked.

He nodded, face still twisted.

"Continue to eat and drink." She turned to go back inside.

"Will you still serve as my guide?" he asked.

She snorted.

"Will you?" He stood up.

She said nothing.

"Will you still kill me when all of this is done?"

For a few seconds, Eris did not move. Then, quick as a snake, she whipped around and slapped him. Vasethe's head snapped sideways. He froze, eyes wide. Something about his stillness made Eris step backwards, her hand still raised.

Then his smile faltered, and he rubbed his cheek where she had struck him.

"Ow," he said, eyes downcast.

"You think that if you tell me everything, I'll refuse to be your guide." She crossed her arms. "Is that right?"

He hesitated. It was enough of an answer.

"Do you know what I believe?"

There was a challenge in her voice and in the set of her jaw. Vasethe could not meet her eyes.

"You aren't trying to bring Raisha back. You came to me to destroy her." Eris continued before he could interrupt. "Or whatever is left of her. And it seems to me that there is a good chance she's the one who left you that scar."

Her word seemed to hit him like a physical force. He shook his head. The imprint of her hand stood out against his skin.

"I think you killed her."

"Stop it."

"But she had a trick up her sleeve, and in her dying breath she cursed you."

"Eris, please *stop*."

"And yet killing her still wasn't enough for you."

"I loved her." Vasethe's voice cracked.

Eris paused.

"I loved her," he croaked. He shook his head again, his eyes shining and haunted. "She got *sick*. Don't you dare . . . You don't . . ."

Eris watched him.

"You have no idea what she was like," he whispered.

"This is ridiculous. Even if you want to destroy her, it's nothing to me."

"Then let's go. Right now."

"You need to recover."

"I don't care," he said.

There was a brief silence.

"I don't," he repeated, more quietly.

Eris let out a long, irritated breath but softened. "Vasethe, you're going to end up permanently damaging your soul. Crossing again so soon borders on suicidal. Tiba managed to loosen the hex's hold, but she couldn't unravel it. If anything goes wrong, I won't be able to absorb the malice."

He shrugged.

"Don't shrug at me," she snapped.

"I already know what you're telling me."

"Then you have a funny way of showing it. If you must kill yourself, at least do it in a way that allows your soul to cross to Mkalis."

"What does it matter to you?"

"Look, much as I want you gone, I don't want to see you annihilated." Eris ran her hands over her hair, crushing it down. "It's your choice, but we could give it time. She can wait. She would want you to wait."

The ghost of a smile touched the corners of his mouth. "Thank you, but I've inconvenienced you for too long already."

Her face closed off. "Yes. I suppose you have."

"What happened to your shoulder?" he asked quietly.

"A ward shattered."

"Last night?" He frowned. "How many are there now?"

"Five. Five out of the eight."

"Why do they keep coming?"

She looked up at him.

"It's not my place to ask," he said. "Sorry."

"He hates me," she said. "That's all. He wants to destroy me and won't stop until he has succeeded."

Vasethe touched her arm lightly. The deadness was fading from his face, the shadows losing hold. Eris gazed at his hand, then shrugged him off.

"If you won't wait," she said, "then we'll go."

Chapter Eleven

THE ROOM WAS COOL and dark. Through the window, Vasethe could see a flat plane of pale grey clouds. Early morning, judging by the light. He sat up and pushed aside the deerskin throw covering him.

The maggots were gone. He probed the raw flesh of his throat. The wound no longer felt feverishly hot and the surrounding skin had calmed, the inflammation negligible. Numb to the touch; it seemed that Eris was still absorbing the malice. Guilt twisted in his gut.

A circular rug of interwoven feathers covered the floor. The down was ticklish beneath his bare feet. He had no memory of this place, but it looked like it might be part of Tiba's realm. Water percolated along the moss-covered walls and collected in the gutters at their base, channelled to a drain in the corner. Apart from the bed, the room held no furniture.

Vasethe walked to the window. Outside, the trees cast shadowy reflections across the surface of the lake. He was inside one of the ribs, in a room carved from bone. Voices and far-off laughter floated up to him; the inhabitants of

Tiba's realm going about their business. In the distance, he could see smoke rising from other settlements along the lake. Strange shapes protruded from the undulating hills. Skulls and femurs, the scattered remains of Tiba's adversaries.

A tap on the door. When Vasethe opened it, Lanesh stood outside.

"Honoured guest, the border keeper and Res Tiba await your presence at the gateway to Buyak's realm." He bowed. "I would also like to convey my sincere apologies for the discomfort you experienced during this detour."

"No need to apologise." Vasethe glanced back into the room. "Would you happen to know where I can find clothes?"

Lanesh scuttled past Vasethe's legs. He flattened himself against the ground, squeezed under the bed and emerged holding a folded bundle between his pincers.

"Your shoes are outside. Covering one's feet inside the ribs is prohibited." He held up the clothes.

"Thanks." Vasethe took his shirt and pulled it over his head. "Anything exciting happen while we were in Ahri?"

"To the best of my knowledge, no. In fairness, I spent most of the time keeping watch outside the border keeper's door. That corridor was probably not representative of Mkalis as a whole."

Vasethe laughed. "Probably not."

He followed Lanesh out of the door. A spiralling metal stairway ran down the heart of the rib, lit by round jars of slow-burning resin. Water droplets echoed all around. When they reached the bottom of the stairs, Vasethe found his boots standing beside the crescent-shaped entrance to the rib. He pulled them on.

Their rowboat was docked outside, swaying in the stream. Tiba's dwellers had vanished again. Apart from the sounds of cicadas and frogs, the settlement was quiet. Vasethe untied the rope and stepped down into the boat. Lanesh hopped aboard behind him.

"You seem better," the crab said.

Vasethe picked up the oars. "Which way?"

"Through there."

He angled one oar against the side of the rib and used it to propel the craft forward. "I feel cleaner."

Lanesh shifted. "The border keeper appeared better too, although I would not presume to know her that well."

"I'm glad to hear that."

"You will have to judge for yourself. You do know her well, I take it?"

Lanesh was not looking at Vasethe, instead watching the thatch-roofed houses slide by. But for the first time since returning to Mkalis, Vasethe noticed the change to the crab's carapace. Lanesh's shell rippled and bulged, like the child had tried to claw its way free.

"Not that well," he replied.

"What is your relationship to her?"

Lanesh's tone was too casual.

"I asked her for help in finding someone. She agreed."

"She seems to be expending a great deal of effort in helping you."

Vasethe did not respond, which appeared to frustrate Lanesh. The crab's pincers clenched and relaxed; he stepped from foot to foot.

"I must admit, I am curious—" he began.

"I don't want to talk about Eris. If you wouldn't mind." Vasethe smiled pleasantly.

Lanesh flinched, his eyes darting to the entrances of shadowy dwellings and slender alleys. The clouds above the trees were tinted salmon pink, the sun rising.

"Lanesh, are you okay?"

He did not reply.

Vasethe rowed the boat into the wider channel and allowed the current to steer it towards a slab of dark stone, where Eris and Tiba stood waiting. Tiba looked calmer than before, and tired. Her braids were bunched into a bun and she was talking to Eris. Their conversation ended when he climbed ashore.

"Thank you for healing me," Vasethe said.

The demon inclined her head. "I did as much as I

could. Don't let my efforts go to waste." She glanced at Lanesh, still in the boat, and then looked back to Vasethe. "Be careful."

He nodded.

"Creature of Buyak," she called. "You may move."

Lanesh bowed and clambered ashore, hurrying over to Vasethe's side.

"This gateway leads to the Leshato Steppe of Buyak's realm," Tiba said, gesturing towards stairs cut down into the rock slab. "From there, it is two days' walk to Demi Anath, the heart of his realm. May the benevolence of the First shelter you."

Eris's smile was wry. "How archaic. Try to stay out of trouble, Tiba."

"Of course," the demon murmured. "Remember our agreement."

The stairs were damp and their base obscured by shadow. Vasethe sighed and found his way to the wall, using it to guide him forward. Lanesh passed him, more at home in the dark. Daylight faded.

"All-powerful border keeper?" Vasethe called.

"What?"

"A torch would be helpful."

She grunted. A moment later, the stairs became visible. There was no discernible source of light, but Vasethe could now see through the gloom. He let go of the lichen-coated wall.

"Thanks." He moved forward. "What agreement was Tiba talking about?"

"Nothing you need to worry about."

"I wouldn't say I'm worried. A little curious, though. And who is the First?"

She made a noise of exasperation. "I agreed to take custody of Tiba's realm if anything happened to her."

"Meaning?"

"*Someone* might not approve of her talking to me. If she dies, I'll find the individual responsible and claim the realm back from them. By force." She reached the base of the stairs and ran her fingers over the wall. "Tiba is very protective of her dwellers."

"Wouldn't that make you a ruler?"

"I already am." She turned, her tone a little defensive.

"Oh."

"Well, I'm more of a caretaker, I suppose." She still looked edgy. "I operate as the custodian of a number of realms, but there are also two that I have claimed. Not with a public declaration or anything. But they're still mine."

"Is that, well, allowed? For a border keeper?"

"It isn't technically forbidden."

Vasethe laughed.

"Oh, shut up."

"How do you claim a realm?"

"Murder whoever rules it. Or inherit, but that's more complicated. And there are rare occasions where a ruler dies of natural causes and leaves their realm unclaimed." She shrugged. "Then it's the same as setting a rule. You speak through blood. 'This is mine now; begone, fools.'"

"I'd like to see your realms someday."

"Am I your tour guide?"

He smiled. "So, who is the First, then?"

"The First is the ruler of the first realm. She's been ..." Eris trailed off, looking past him. "Lanesh?"

The child's hand had cracked the surface of the carapace. The crab was shaking even as he walked, his eyestalks shuddering.

"Stop," Lanesh whispered. "Don't cross. You don't understand."

"What's happening?" Vasethe demanded.

Lanesh made an odd keening noise and came to a halt. Vasethe took a step towards him.

"Stop," Lanesh repeated. His carapace rippled and shivered, the child writhing beneath the shell. The crack widened.

"Vasethe, get Tiba. Now," Eris said.

"They have a God Compass already," Lanesh hissed. "Buyak wants you to think—" He convulsed and liquid seeped from his mouth. "Forge ... God Sword ... to cut—"

"Who is 'they'?" Eris demanded.

Lanesh stopped speaking and froze. Eris snarled and lunged towards him, but it was useless. With a crunching, grinding sound, Lanesh began to shrink. Bright red blood leaked from the joints between his carapace and his legs, bubbled out from his eyes and antennae.

Vasethe was rooted to the spot.

Lanesh never made a sound. He just continued to shrink, down, down, down, till his shell was no larger than a child's toy, and the floor was awash with gore. Only then did he lower his pincers.

They both stood and stared at the crab.

"Lanesh?" Vasethe whispered.

Eris knelt. The crab ran in a circle before scuttling towards her palm. She picked it up. "In a way, this is a mercy," she muttered. She pressed a single finger to the creature's buckled carapace and it dissolved into dust. "Rulers have almost absolute control over their subjects," she said. "To abuse or to care for, to love or to slaughter." She opened her hands and the dust drifted away. "But they cannot control what resides within their hearts."

Vasethe balled his hands into fists. "Buyak did this?"

"Of course." She stood up and gazed down the tunnel. "And Lanesh expected no less. Welcome to Mkalis. I suppose it is true after all; I have been gone for far too long."

"We should have done something."

"Done what?" She turned. "Come on."

He could not see her face, only the stiffness of her narrow shoulders. she started walking.

He followed her.

Chapter Twelve

THE BEACH SLOPED UPWARDS to merge with pale dunes, the sand dotted with grass and clusters of fat blue aloes. Behind them, the ocean continued its heavy sway. The high tide lapped at the entrance to the Hollow Way, water draining into the passages with each wave.

Vasethe shivered. The sun was just rising over the golden water, and the damp sand crunched beneath his feet. After walking so long in the close, stale tunnels, the air felt raw in his mouth. He tucked his hands into his armpits to keep them warm.

Eris had hardly spoken since Lanesh's death, but the way that she moved was different. Driven. Vasethe walked a little way behind her, studying the lines of her shoulders as she strode up the dune. Her feet did not sink into the fine sand and left only shallow imprints in her wake. Even in the half-light, her crystalline freckles shone against the darkness of her skin. It was strange, the way she seemed to exude a light of her own. As she reached the top of the last dune, the sunrise caught her hair and it blazed orange. She turned to check on him.

Vasethe quickly looked away.

The dunes gave way to dusty scrubland. Coral-pink proteas rustled in the breeze. All across the plain, the sun-scorched prows of sunken ships jutted up from the hard-baked earth. A few still had masts and tattered sails, the yellowed canvas flapping in the wind.

"So, this is the Leshato Steppe." Vasethe shaded his eyes against the sun. "Have you been here before?"

"No."

The closest ship was only around fifty paces from the dunes. Skulls lined the gunwales, grinning sightlessly. As they neared the vessel, Vasethe heard the faint sound of jovial fiddling.

"Stay close," called Eris. Vasethe hurried to catch up with her.

Bright-scaled lizards sat atop rocks, drinking in the early sun. They scattered as he passed. With each step, the orange dust of the steppe stained his boots.

"Eris?"

She kept walking.

"What did he mean by 'God Compass'?"

She was silent for so long that he thought she would not answer.

"Are you familiar with God Instruments?" she asked at last.

"I don't think so."

"A God Compass can track powerful souls and allows its bearer to cross realms without permissions." Her voice was dispassionate. "During the War of Black Sand, Kan Imasu of the 67th realm was successful in creating one. Using it, she hunted down and slaughtered ninety members of the Demonic Concord."

"And now there might be another one?"

"Possibly. Forging any Instrument is taboo because their creation disrupts the circulation of life between Ahri and Mkalis. God Instruments are shaped from souls willingly forfeited, tempered in the lifeblood of a conquered ruler."

"Willingly forfeited? In Umbakur, the lanterns in the corridor referred to a forge."

"I saw," she said shortly. "Buyak and I need to talk."

A skull dropped from the gunwale and landed with a clatter on the arid soil. Vasethe stared up at the ship.

"Is something wrong?"

The figurehead gazed down at him with sun-bleached eyes, lips parted hungrily. Her nose had snapped off.

"I'm not sure," he said.

"Keep moving."

He nodded. The wind swelled, and the ships groaned in chorus; their sails fluttered and twisted. Music drifted from the hulls, soft but increasing in volume. As they passed a half-submerged brig, Vasethe glimpsed movement through the portholes.

Da-dum.

The drum fell silent again, one heartbeat in a grave-yard. Eris gestured for him to stop.

The creature emerged from a splintered cavity in the hull. It stood around Vasethe's height, back bowed by the weight of its huge head, steps apelike and teetering. Two rows of steel spines protruded from its white brow, and two eyes glinted in their sunken sockets. It lumbered forward, violin in hand, sawing the strings with vigour. No mouth, no nose or ears that Vasethe could see. Masses of densely curled black fur covered its heavy limbs, leaving only elegant human hands and a smooth, bone-white visage exposed.

"State your purpose, realm dweller," said Eris.

It played on, advancing towards them. With a growl, Eris raised one hand and the creature froze. Although its fingers had stopped moving, the music did not falter. Another creature emerged from the hull.

"I have no desire to harm you," Eris told the frozen musician. "But neither will I hesitate to."

"More are coming," Vasethe said, watching the other ships. From beneath the ground, he could hear the sound of drums.

"Buyak's got a death wish," Eris snarled.

A second later, she cried out and doubled over. Pain

lanced through Vasethe's throat.

"Eris?" he gasped.

She spat blood. "Sorry, Sethe. Seems that I lied. How many are there?"

"At least twelve."

The first musician was nearly upon them. Eris gestured and it slid backwards, freezing again.

"More than I would like." She paralysed the next creature. Vasethe shielded her back.

The violinist twitched under Eris's spell, fighting the binding. Music poured from the ships, bright and cheery and unrelenting, all perfectly in key, as synchronised as an orchestra. Dark figures wove across the steppe, steps falling in time to the deep vibrations of hidden drums. *Da-da-dum-da, da-da-dum-da.* Regular, insistent.

"Draw on your power," Vasethe said.

"No."

"Then at least arm me with something."

"Quiet."

The violinist pushed the bow across the instrument's strings, one sheer note, and froze again. Vasethe could now count twenty musicians, all inching towards them. Eris's breathing was heavy.

She slashed her arm through the air. The violinist crumbled into ash. The violin fell to the ground and the music faltered.

"Any more takers?" she called.

Da-da-dum, da-da-dum. The song recommenced with vigour.

"Let's move." She stepped forward.

"We're surrounded," he said.

Eris swore.

"Let the hex revert to me for a few seconds."

"I told you to be quiet."

"Just do it!"

"No."

Eris incinerated another musician and Vasethe's throat burned. The music paused, gathered again, swelled.

"I can handle it," he said. "Please."

She ignored him.

The drumming resonated within his diaphragm. He crouched and snatched up a stone. The creatures moved quicker now, waltzing towards them. Vasethe threw the rock at a flutist. The missile bounced harmlessly off the creature's shoulder and hit the instrument, producing a discordant note. The music paused.

Vasethe glanced at Eris.

"I'm going to try something," she said.

She swept her arms outwards and sent the musicians stumbling back. Then she inhaled, as if to dive underwater, and sang.

Her voice soared over the ships, wrenching through

the creatures' orderly rhythms with a penetrating, erratic sound, wordless and angry and demanding. The musicians halted, their fingers hovering over frets and strings.

A vicious grin played across Eris's face. Still singing, she grasped Vasethe's wrist and dragged him forward through the maze of ships. The strange creatures were unable to move; they twitched like the hands of a stopped clock, their bodies turning to track Eris's progress through their midst. The steppe stretched for miles, offering no shelter, only sparse grey vegetation and lone, leafless trees. Eris sang on, undaunted. The sunken leviathans groaned as if battered by her voice.

A high-pitched bellow rang out over the plain.

"What is that?" asked Vasethe.

Eris tightened her grip around Vasethe's wrist. Her voice cracked and the musicians lunged towards them, lightning quick, but she recovered and they froze.

Seven figures appeared in the distance, raising a storm of dust in their wake. Riders on top of strange animals. They streaked across the steppe at breakneck pace.

Eris stopped and shoved Vasethe behind her.

A rider whooped. Their mounts were huge and armoured, bird-faced creatures the size of bears, with two thick legs and cloven hooves. The animals produced high yips like a pack of feral dogs, and their riders wore horned skull masks draped with strings of multicoloured beads and copper wire and quartz. Bars of dark red paste streaked their arms.

The rider at the head of the pack pulled sharply on her reins, and the mount skidded to a stop in front of Eris. Behind her, another rider blew on a curved horn.

"Quickly," she said, voice muffled by her mask, "Come with us."

Eris kept singing.

Vasethe's mouth was dry. "State your purpose, realm dweller."

"I am Tyn, Second Spear of the retinue of Res Lfae, Ruler of the 194th Realm. My current 'purpose' is to rescue a pair of travellers from a grisly death." She tugged on the reins, causing her mount to bank to the right, and offered him a hand. "Now move."

Vasethe looked at Eris. She nodded. He grasped the stranger's wrist and she pulled him up behind her. Muscles corded her wiry arms. She wheeled her animal around, and Vasethe grabbed hold of her waist.

Eris's voice faltered again and the pause was enough. The musicians recommenced their brash music, louder and fiercer than before. The ground thrummed with the force of the unseen drummers. She whirled around to face them and pushed the creatures away with a furious gesture. A second rider rushed up to her, leaning far out of his saddle, and swept her onto his animal.

Tyn ululated and her mount leapt forward. Then they were flying across the scrubland.

Other riders whooped and cheered, egging their animals on. The mounts thundered across the steppe, breathtakingly fast. Tyn crouched low in the saddle. The way she moved, she could have been an extension of the creature's body.

Without warning, they veered left and Vasethe lost his grip. The ground raced up to meet him, but Tyn reached out and caught him by the back of his shirt. She pulled him upright.

"Easy there," she said.

He swallowed hard. "Thanks."

"Don't tuck your elbows in; it makes it harder to balance."

He adjusted his posture.

"Better."

It did not feel any better to Vasethe, but he kept his arms up anyway. The other riders veered and shifted, jostling for a place at the head of the pack. Their skull masks leered at him. He caught sight of Eris through the fray.

"Want to see what Pax can really do?" Tyn asked over her shoulder. She wasn't even looking at the terrain ahead and her mount navigated its own way. Eyes glinted through the slits of her mask.

"What?"

Tyn laughed and the wind whipped her long hair across his face. She crouched lower in the saddle, leaned forward, and spoke into her mount's ear. The animal's muscles rippled beneath Vasethe.

The motion wrenched him by the arms and he swore. Their mount surged ahead; the world blurred around them, an impression of brush and earth and sky. Tyn laughed. Every part of Vasethe sang with adrenaline: the world alight with brighter colours, the sound of the mount's hooves magnified in his ears, a second heartbeat. Everything was clear.

They raced on, heading for the distant hills, towards a thin plume of smoke rising in the air.

Chapter Thirteen

TYN SLOWED HER MOUNT at the base the ochre cliffs. Out of sight, water gurgled. The air was sharp with the smell of vegetation.

"We will meet up with Res Lfae at the pass," she said, slightly out of breath.

The other riders were specks on the horizon, shimmering in the haze. Vasethe wiped sweat from his forehead. The sun was at its height; when Tyn had offered him a drink, he almost accepted before remembering the rules.

Tyn led her mount, Pax, through a thicket of thorn bushes, and they emerged beside a shallow rivulet. The animal bent and drank.

"She's the second-fastest d'wen in the pack," Tyn said with affection. "Bad-tempered but loyal. Isn't that right, grouchy?"

Pax chittered.

Vasethe patted the animal's haunch. Its feathers were the colour of sand and surprisingly soft. "Thank you for coming to our aid."

"Res Lfae told us to. So, that was the border keeper back there?"

"Yes."

"Hm. Apparently, she and my ruler are old friends. That makes you . . ."

He shrugged. "My name is Vasethe."

Tyn worked at the knot that held her skull mask in place. "I'm guessing you're from Ahri, given that you don't want to drink."

"Astute."

She was tall and lithe. Her skin was covered with intricate tattoos: illegible writing, letters entwined with birds, with vines and flames and water. "Who are you looking for?"

"I never said I was looking for anyone."

"Yeah, but that's generally why Ahrians come to Mkalis, isn't it?" She removed the mask and set it on a rock. She had hawkish features, a nose that had broken and healed skew. "If the old stories are anything to go by, you should be here to track down some helpless lover and drag them kicking and screaming back to Ahri."

He snorted.

"No?"

"No."

Tyn splashed her face with water and slicked back her hair. In the distance, Vasethe could hear the sound of hooves. Pax raised her head and looked towards the noise. She barked and the pack answered.

"Patience, you silly creature." Tyn retrieved her mask and hoisted herself back into the saddle. She offered Vasethe her hand. "Are you heading to Demi Anath?"

"That's the plan."

She tapped Pax's ribs. The animal grumbled and turned around. "Perhaps you can travel with us."

"Us?"

"My tribe and the rest of the retinue from the 194th realm. Domain of Res Lfae, One Who Wields the Machete, Marquis of the Spine Light"—she gestured theatrically as she rattled off the titles—"and partygoer of note."

Vasethe smiled. "I'd like the company, but it's Eris's call."

"She will be in for a long, hot walk if she declines."

They left the thicket and emerged into sunlight. The other riders were only a few hundred feet away; Tyn waved to them and they slowed. The d'wens panted and crooned.

"You'll exhaust your animal," one of the riders called.

"I wanted to stretch her legs," Tyn replied.

"Apparently, she needs stretching every hour or so."

Sounds of general amusement. Vasethe caught Eris's eye. She looked tired.

Having fun? Her voice inside his head caught him by surprise, and she smiled.

"Honoured border keeper," Tyn said, in a more formal tone, "please forgive me for the rushed introductions earlier. My ruler is waiting for us to rejoin the caravans at the base of the Jifui Pass. It is not too far from here and you are welcome to accompany us."

"Good," said Eris. "I'd like to talk to Lfae anyway."

The riders were relaxed and talked amongst themselves; some removed their masks. Relaxed but still dangerous. Strapped to the d'wens' saddles were spears and crossbows, scimitars with stained blades, and battered shields. They looked ready to ride into battle. White-barked quiver trees dotted the cliffs, casting stiff black shadows across the ground. A lappet-faced vulture swung lazy arcs through the sky.

"Have you been to Demi Anath before?" Vasethe asked Tyn.

"Not personally, no, but some of my tribespeople have seen it. 'The City of Inverted Waters.' I expect it will be quite impressive." She swatted an insect. "Although I doubt it will rival my ruler's cities."

"I suspect you might be biased."

"I suspect you might be right." She pointed at the cliffs ahead. "Here we are."

Vasethe leaned sideways in the saddle. A giant crack

split the rock face at the end of the valley, and at the base of the cliffs stood a host of covered wagons. One of the riders behind them blew their horn. An answering blast echoed across the steppe, accompanied by a cacophony of barking.

"Hale, Thethametsu, Saa, Koitu, take your d'wens to drink," said Tyn. "Nthu, Matir, come with me."

Eris's rider urged his mount forward. Another man, his chipped skull mask resting on his lap, did likewise. The others turned and made for the stream.

Enormous bird nests festooned the shaded interior of the crack in the rock face, the walls streaked with white droppings. As they approached, Vasethe felt a cool wind blowing through the cleft. The d'wens sidestepped nervously.

"They are edgier than usual," said Eris's rider, his voice a low rumble.

Tyn shot him a glare. He shrugged.

"They've never liked the dark," she said, after a moment.

"It's not that dark in there. They smell something."

"Enough, Matir."

He fell silent.

The caravans were draped in coloured silks and decorated with painted skulls and wire antennae. There were fifteen wagons in total, harnessed to giant horned beetles.

The beetles appeared foul-tempered, tossing their heads and pawing at the ground. Minders scratched their backs with long sticks and wafted smoke towards them with large fans.

"Hey, Upstart!" A woman strode towards them. She addressed Tyn. "Where is everyone else?"

Tyn dismounted. "They're just behind me. The d'wens were thirsty." She tucked her mask into the crook of one arm.

"Res Lfae has been waiting for you."

"I know."

Vasethe slid off Pax. His legs were stiff and unsteady.

"Border keeper, this is First Spear Vehn," said Tyn.

The woman bowed smoothly from the waist. "I apologize for not assisting you myself, your Reverence. I had been scouting the pass, so Res Lfae sent the Second Spear in my place." She motioned for two youths to collect the mounts. "May I take you directly to my ruler?"

"Please do." Eris climbed down. Her voice sounded in Vasethe's head. *Lfae was amongst Yett's closest allies. As rulers go, one of my favourites.*

"Are you allowed favourites?" he muttered to her.

I do what I like. She followed Vehn and nodded politely to Tyn in farewell. *It's well known that we're friends, so nobody has tried to invade Lfae's realm in centuries.*

Vasethe stepped out of the way to let the d'wen pass.

Tyn threw him a lazy salute and headed for a striped red caravan with Matir.

"Stay out of trouble," she called.

"I'll try."

Flies buzzed. Vasethe caught up with Eris and Vehn. Members of Lfae's retinue lolled around in the shade of their caravans, their faces dyed in brilliant hues by the reflected light of the silk.

Vehn stopped in front of a green and gold caravan and stood to attention.

"Res Lfae?" she called. "The border keeper is here."

Vasethe heard rustling, and the silk was swept aside.

The demon was tall and slender, with platinum hair that fell in soft waves to the ground. The strength of their jaw was offset by the delicacy of their mouth, and their age was indeterminate. Young, old, male, female, Vasethe could not tell. The light soaked into their honey-coloured features, and they seemed at once alien and kind, warm and regal. Their deep hazel eyes met his, and Vasethe had the sense that the demon knew every secret he had ever kept.

Eris nudged him in the ribs. "Close your mouth."

Vasethe shut his mouth.

"I do enjoy watching the effect I have on the unsuspecting." Lfae's voice was like a wind instrument in early morning mist. "Hello, mortal."

Vasethe made a garbled sound.

"Oh, get a grip, Sethe." Eris was grinning. "Long time no see, Lfae. Thank you for the assistance."

The demon motioned for her to come inside, wrists tinkling with silver jewellery. "So nice to see you again. I worry about you, Midan."

"Not Midan anymore."

"Still. I worry."

"I'm sure you have better things to do with your time." Eris entered the caravan.

"You look tired."

"You didn't have to say so."

Vasethe followed them inside. He felt dazed.

The interior held an eclectic mix of weapons, sheaves of paper, and embroidered cushions. A mobile hung overhead; the rusted contraption dangling heavy iron orbs on rings.

Eris flopped down on a pile of cushions. Lfae let the silk cover fall shut, blocking out the burning sunlight.

"Can we be heard?" she asked, more seriously.

"By Buyak?" Lfae smirked. "What do you take me for?"

The demon's shining hair had fallen over Vasethe's boot. He wasn't sure whether moving his foot would be disrespectful.

"Oh, stop toying with him," said Eris.

Lfae pulled their hair aside. "You spoil my fun."

"So, it's secure here?"

"Only my own people can hear us in here, but the realm's rules obviously still apply, so, you know, don't lie."

"I've already learned that lesson the hard way."

"Really? It's unlike you to be careless." The demon reclined. "How much do you know?"

Eris shrugged. "Hard to say. I've heard a few rumours."

"So, you know about Kstille?"

"That he's missing. And he may have had an argument with Buyak."

"Oh, he did; I was present at that meeting. He called for a Tribunal."

"Did he say why?"

Lfae adjusted the cushions. "Not in my hearing, but there are only a few valid grounds for a call. So, I would guess he believed God Instruments were involved. I might even guess that Kstille's vanishing coincided with the appearance of a new trinket somewhere in the realms."

"That's my assumption. I am reasonably sure that a new Compass has been forged." She scowled. "And I have heard that a Sword is next."

Lfae's eyes widened. "I did not know *that.*"

"I could have been misled, but I doubt it. Plus, there's the return of the Ageless, just as this man appeared on my doorstep."

Lfae's gaze hardened. The weapons on the walls gleamed, and Vasethe suddenly had the sense that something invisible, sharp, and poisonous was pressed to his throat.

"Stop that," Eris snapped.

"My apologies," Lfae said, although their eyes did not move.

"I trust him. I think he is being used, but I trust him. Lfae, don't make me tell you again. Stop."

The demon paused for a heartbeat longer, then the atmosphere inside the caravan lifted. "Whatever you say."

Vasethe tried to control his face and breathing.

I trust him.

"But I lied," he said softly.

"Sethe?"

"I didn't want to tell you, because I needed you as my guide. I was scared you would withdraw your aid."

"What are you talking about?"

"You asked whether I saw anyone in the minor realm. There was a woman. She knew who I was." He spoke quickly. "She knew that you would come for me."

"What?"

"Eris, I was wrong—"

"'Eris?'" Lfae interrupted. "You call her 'Eris'? Why would you do that? No wonder the Ageless have returned."

"What does her name have to do with anything?"

"We are not discussing that," Eris said.

Her voice was raw. The wagon fell silent.

"Go on," she said. "What else?"

Vasethe tried to meet her eyes, but she stared past him. "The woman said that I was exactly where she wanted me to be."

"I don't follow."

Her coldness cut him. "Doesn't it seem like we've been pushed into following a certain path through the realms? I think Buyak wanted you to talk to Tiba. I think he wanted you to know about Kstille. And I think he's working with this woman."

More than anything, he wished she would look at him.

"I think we're walking into a trap," he whispered.

"Are you finished?" asked Eris.

Her eyes shone, and she would not look up.

"Go back to Ahri," she said.

Before he could protest, she leaned over, pressed her hand to his chest, and sent him from Mkalis.

Chapter Fourteen

VASETHE WOKE. His heart beat slow and calm; Eris's hand on his chest was light as air. Everything seemed weightless. He felt he could drift right off the bed, rise into space. Golden dust motes floated through the doorway. They hung in the still air, slow as the movement of stars.

"Eris?"

Her breath stirred the fine hairs on his arm.

"I'm sorry," he whispered.

Eris's breathing changed as she returned to her Ahri body. Her fingers twitched and air escaped her mouth in a low sigh. When she sat up, he thought she would speak. Instead, she rose from the bed in a rustle of sheets and left the room.

Vasethe rubbed his eyes. He stood, tied his hair up, and straightened out the covers. In the mirror, he looked younger, more innocent, vulnerable in the afternoon glow.

Eris was not in the house or the yard. The desert beyond her fence stretched away to eternity. Vasethe moved from room to room, but she was gone.

He sat beneath the awning. For a long time, he waited, staring out to the horizon. So quiet. It struck him that his old professors had been wrong; the edge of the world was not an ocean.

When it grew dark, he lit the lantern in the front room. He found his chisels and, within the ring of lamplight, he carved. He worked fine details into the rich, gleaming wood of the table and smoothed away rough edges with a mixture of sand and oil. The stars shone bright; the dust of other universes drifted unobserved above the house.

He completed it. It should have been varnished, but her words lingered in his mind. Bodies decomposed slowly around here. Let it rot if she wanted it to rot; he would not drag out the decay. Let her forget him sooner.

If she wanted it to endure, it would.

Vasethe set the table beneath the lantern and collected his pack. His gourds were full; the water would last until he reached Shanan. He only took dried meat from Eris's cupboard, and even that felt like an imposition. The taste in his mouth was bitter and gritty, like he had breathed in sawdust while carving. He closed the door behind him but did not extinguish the light.

The latch on the gate was stuck. He worked it free. The waning moon had risen above the saltpan, lighting his way. The more distance he covered before sunrise, the better. Vasethe rolled his shoulders, refusing to look back.

The wards shivered. The moon dimmed.

He turned towards the shadowline.

Seven figures stood on the saltpan, grotesque scarecrows outlined by moonlight. All still as death, all staring towards the house. The eighth Ageless was a distant silhouette.

"Leave her alone!" shouted Vasethe.

They did not react. He pulled the knife from his boot. The creatures reminded him of something, but their presence made it difficult to think. The shadowline hummed, a high-pitched whine that made his ears ache. The wards thrummed along Eris's fence.

Vasethe threw his knife. His aim was perfect; it should have hit the centre Ageless right between the eyes. But the blade disappeared the moment it crossed the shadowline, evaporating in a shower of salt crystals.

Vasethe blinked and the Ageless were looking at him. He stumbled forward—was pulled forward—catching himself a few feet from the line. This close, he could smell them, crypt dust and rotted flesh. Their white eyes did not move.

He felt sleepy, even as his brain screamed for him to back away. There was a majesty, almost an arrogance to the Ageless. Before them, he was nothing, a fleeting life, already dead, decomposing, a small, passing thing.

Something unseen coiled around his chest and yanked him backwards. He landed hard and the air *whoosh*ed from his lungs.

"You idiot," said Eris.

She stood above him. Her arm was bloodied and her shift torn. Although her eyes were red, she looked calm. Blood dripped from her fingers onto the sand.

"Get inside the fence. Now," she said.

Another wound opened on her leg, the skin peeling away like a flower blooming.

"Eris—"

"Now."

She sighed as the latch on the gate clicked shut.

"My wards will hold here," she said wearily. "He has a limited ability to warp the space close to the shadow-line, but he can't cross it without a direct and sustained assault."

"Your wounds . . ."

"So, you're going to walk away from Raisha, then?"

He flinched.

"I don't care," she said. "I just wonder why you bothered to waste my time in the first place, if you're prepared to quit like this."

"I was never looking for Raisha."

Silence.

"She died six years ago," he said.

"You . . . what?"

"It wasn't that I lacked the desperation back then. And I knew it might be possible." His throat was tight. "It was her research project: *Interpreting Non-Pol Accounts of the Incarnations of the Border Keeper following the Demonic War.* I took it over after her death." He looked away. "I knew that resurrecting her was possible."

Eris stared at him.

"She—she wouldn't have wanted—" He shook his head. "It's done now; I'm leaving. I swear that I never meant you any harm."

"Sethe, stop."

Eris reached out and steadied herself against him. Her fingers were slick with burning blood.

"Help me inside," she muttered. "Please? I can't stand."

She was heavier than he expected. He shouldered the door open. His skin blistered where it pressed against her injured arm and leg, the fabric of his shirt disintegrating.

He set her down on the ground and hurried to the kitchen. He filled a large bowl with water, retrieved a bottle of brandy and rolls of bandages from the trunk in the corner.

Eris was lying flat on her back when he returned, staring at the ceiling. He knelt at her side and carefully pressed a damp sponge to the gash on her arm.

"Medicine," she said. "You said you studied it for a while."

He rinsed away the blood. There was little risk of infection, but he did not take chances. To her credit, Eris did not even wince when he poured a measure of the brandy over the wound.

"High pain tolerance, huh?" she said, watching him.

Vasethe riffled through his pack until he found his needle. His hands steady, he dipped it in brandy then threaded it.

"The worst part is that I had just told Lfae I trusted you." She watched as he pushed the needle through her skin. "So embarrassing. There will be centuries of ridicule to look forward to."

He wiped away blood and brandy, continued stitching. His fingertips seared, but he did not pause.

"From the moment you arrived, I knew that you were testing me, manipulating me. And yet I let you get away with it." She laughed. "I suppose this is really my own fault."

He shook his head.

"Come, don't look so sad. You're much prettier when you smile."

"You're hurt," he said quietly, "and I'm responsible."

"You give yourself too much credit," she said. She

peered at her arm to check his progress. "Very tidy, though."

Vasethe finished and cut the thread. He sponged the wound and pressed a strip of gauze over the cut. Then he unwound a bandage with his other hand and set about wrapping up her arm.

"After Raisha's death," he said, voice barely louder than a whisper, "I moved from Utyl to Kisfath. I needed a job, so I applied to the St. Hsa Avatarium. I was accepted into the trade."

She said nothing.

"Three years later, I was sent to Chenash. It's a small community, and I was the only avatar there. The place was unusually conservative, but I managed; I had regulars, including a woman named Nialle." He pinned the bandage, lifted her arm to ensure she could still move it easily. "For about a year, everything was fine. I hoped to earn enough to travel, maybe go north to join the survey crew on the Miame border. But then Nialle's baby went missing."

Eris caught his wrist when he moved the needle towards her leg. "I'll do it."

"No, I can manage."

She took the needle and thread from him. "Your fingers are burnt enough. Wash your hands." She pushed the bowl of water towards him. "And refill that."

He did as she said. The Ageless were gone. He let his hands rest in the kitchen sink and stared out at the moonlit desert.

"When Nialle's husband summoned me to his forge, I went. He was the ordained ysfer of Chenash and crafted all the temple's sacred ornaments. Well respected."

Vasethe returned to the front room and put the bowl down by Eris's side. He opened his mouth to speak but hesitated, struggling to find the words. Eris washed blood away from the ugly wound on her leg, much rougher than he had been.

"He—well, I hadn't expected trouble. I assumed that he condoned Nialle's attendance to the St. Hsa house. It was stupid of me."

Eris bit off a piece of thread and slipped it through the needle.

"I think I managed to throw one punch before he overpowered me. You know the worst thing? He was crying."

She paused in her stitching.

"Crying the whole time." Vasethe's breathing was shallow. "He had the crucible ready. Molten copper. He was an artist, really; from what I could understand, I'd seduced his wife with a silver tongue. He'd forge something similar in my mouth."

Eris finished with the needle. She dipped her bloodied hands into the bowl and washed them clean. Her sutures were nothing like Vasethe's; the loops of thread were loose and untidy, but the wound was closed. Vasethe dressed her leg with gauze and unrolled another bandage.

"Nialle must have heard the fight. She caught him by surprise and smashed his skull with a hammer. He spilt the copper. Missed my mouth, splashed my neck instead."

His breath caught when Eris reached up and touched the scar on his throat.

"Here?"

He nodded.

She traced her fingertips over the damaged skin, then withdrew her hand. "And then?"

"It's hard to remember. I was fading in and out." He pinned the bandage. "Is that too tight?"

"Not at all." Eris flexed her foot. "Thank you."

Vasethe slipped an arm around her waist and helped her to her feet. "Nialle was there. She had her hands on my chest and kept saying that I needed to find her daughter. I remember that I couldn't speak. There was a hole, I could feel it; I was breathing through it."

"But you survived."

"I shouldn't have." He guided Eris into the bedroom. "When I woke up, I was in the mayor's house. Nialle had performed a leech bond to save me, and killed herself in the process."

"Oh."

He helped her onto the bed. "I still can't understand why she did it."

"So, you want to repay your debt and bring her back?"

"No." Vasethe shook his head. "No, I promised I'd find her daughter."

Understanding dawned on Eris's face.

"Nialle left the cradle unattended, and when she returned, the baby was different," he said.

"Sethe—"

"She swore it wasn't hers anymore," he pressed on. "That someone had taken her child and left another behind. And her husband noticed the change too; not that he came to the same conclusion. He just knew it wasn't *his* daughter."

"Sethe, listen to me. She was wrong." Eris gripped his hand. "That type of thing, it doesn't happen. I don't *let* it happen. Unless through death, no one crosses the shadowline, not gods, not demons, and certainly not stolen infants."

"Then why was the questing successful?"

She stiffened.

"When you performed the questing you found her in the disconnected realm." Vasethe sat on the bed beside her. "She was there."

Eris closed her eyes. For a long time, she did not move. She still had Vasethe's hand; he could feel the calluses on her palms. Then she exhaled slowly.

"I have two questions," she said.

He kept quiet.

"Why didn't you tell me all of this in the first place?"

He tried to smile, but his voice came out ragged. "What, tell the all-knowing border keeper I'm a whore?"

"It's not like that. Why should I care?"

"I've learned that some people do. I would also have had to tell this story, and I really didn't want to. But now I have. Your second question?"

"The obvious one."

"Ask."

Eris frowned. "Sethe . . ."

"Go on."

She sighed. "Is it possible?"

"I took professional precautions, and I don't think so. But it's always possible. Not that it should matter."

"Of course it matters," Eris said.

Her voice was almost gentler than Vasethe could stand.

"I would have come to you, even if there was no chance," he rasped.

"I know." She pulled his arm, drew him closer. "I know you would have."

"I would have still come to you."

She hugged him.

"We'll find her."

Chapter Fifteen

THE WAGON WHEELS BOUNCED up the rock-strewn incline; the beetles strained and hissed. Light filtered through the pale green silk above Vasethe's head. He rubbed his eyes and sat up.

He had tried to dissuade Eris from returning, but she had been adamant.

"Apart from anything else, my influence in Mkalis stems from my reputation," she said. "The rulers need to see me as infallible."

"You're going to gain a reputation for madness. Or stupidity."

She grinned. "They already think I'm mad. But they'll never think I'm stupid."

Outside the wagon he heard shouting and the blasting of a horn. The air was cooler than it had been on the steppe. He peered through the gap in the silks.

They were still inside the fissure, but the exit was ahead—a lightning bolt–shaped crack in the rock. Only one wagon fit through the gap at a time. D'wen riders moved around the wagons, assisting the beetle drivers and keeping watch. Vehn barked orders from the front of the train.

"Demi Anath is just beyond the exit of the pass." Tyn brought Pax around the side of the wagon. She offered Vasethe her hand. "Want to see?"

He grasped her wrist and she pulled him onto her mount.

"Everything okay between you and the border keeper?" she asked under her breath.

"I'm still breathing."

She snorted.

At the mouth of the crevasse, the light grew blinding and Demi Anath rose like a mirage before them. Great towers of sapphire and jade floated in the air, suspended by cascades of water that fell towards the sky. Rainbows danced between the liquid pillars, and white egrets wove between water and stone. Stairways tumbled with vines, and slim walkways traipsed the distance from spire to spire. Closer to the ground, the buildings were smaller and darker. A lush oasis of reeds and pools flourished in the city's shadows.

"The verdict?" Vasethe asked Tyn.

"It satisfies my expectations," she said, with a faint air of reluctance.

"The border keeper has gone on ahead, to request a private audience with Kan Buyak." Lfae reined in a sleek silver d'wen beside Pax and nodded curtly to Vasethe. "We are to meet her at the convocation this evening. You will be attending as one of my spears."

Vasethe nodded.

"The rest of my retinue will rejoin us in the city."

The demon spurred the silver mount down the steep incline. "Come."

Pax tossed her head and followed, finding sure footing amongst the sliding rocks. Demi Anath sat within a depression in the land, surrounded on all sides by cliffs and mountains.

Vasethe looked back at Lfae's retinue, still emerging from the pass. Under Vehn's watchful eye, the first wagon was through. Above her head, the cliff face was carved with thousands of egrets taking flight, individual feathers etched into the stone.

"Vasethe?"

He started and straightened in the saddle. "Yes?"

"What's going on?" Tyn sounded troubled.

"What do you mean?"

"Res Lfae is worried. And angry. We wouldn't normally rush like this, leaving the rest of the retinue behind. I don't like it."

He was quiet for a while. In Ahri, he had told Eris everything he could remember of the minor realm and the conversation he had heard in Umbakur. But if the

border keeper had made sense of it all, she kept her con-
clusions to herself.

"I think someone wants to harm Eris," he said. "But
I don't know how. And I'm worried that I might have
helped them. Might still help them."

Tyn elbowed him. "Have a little faith in yourself. You
can fight back."

By the time they reached the oasis, they found it
bustling with rulers and their attendants. Many-legged
demons flirted with gods of solid silver. A goddess
sprouted acacia thorns from her arms; the breath of a
wizened crone bloomed in flurries of ice. A demon with
poetic verses stitched in black thread across his chest
screamed at a cowering attendant. Swarms of flies
clothed the body of a shaven god; occasionally, he picked
one from his skin and ate it alive.

Lfae motioned for them to dismount at the edge of
the reeds. The demon whispered to the silver-feathered
d'wen, and it chittered, then headed back in the direction
of the caravans. Pax followed.

The sultry air was filled with the whining of jewel-
bellied mosquitoes, their complaints rising above the
gentle hushing of the papyrus. Frogs croaked and
weaver birds swooped to catch insects. A walkway covered in woven mats cut through the reeds, below the
towers.

Lfae moved down it with assurance. No one paid them any attention. Shrieks and moans floated through the reeds, sounds of exaltation or pain. Vasethe found it difficult to tell the difference.

"How many rulers are coming to this convocation?" he muttered to Tyn.

"I'm not sure. Probably the first three hundred. Some rulers have ridiculously large retinues, though."

A marble staircase led up to a broad deck fifty feet in the air.

"Our transport," Lfae announced.

Teams of giant egrets waited on the platform, their talons wrapped around the bars of gilded silver cages. Each cage held two benches, the seats covered in plush green velvet. Tyn looked at the birds doubtfully but climbed inside a cage.

"There are still a few hours until the assembly begins. That leaves us with some time to assess the situation." Lfae stepped into the closest cage and sat down. The ruler's gaze swung towards Vasethe. "Remember not to eat or drink? You'll need to stay focused. When a large group of rulers gather in one place, the effect can be intoxicating."

Looking at the demon directly still made Vasethe dizzy. "I can imagine."

The egrets shook out their feathers. With powerful

downward strokes of their white wings, they took to the air. The cage swayed as it was lifted off the ground, and the oasis dropped away below them. Tyn gripped the sides of the bench and stared straight ahead, her jaw clenched.

"The three of us will attend the opening of the assembly alone," Lfae continued. "You should be ignored, but remain watchful. We want to avoid trouble for now."

The birds swooped between two columns of water, towards a mirror-bright tower of pale orange stone. In the light of the sunset, the unnatural waters turned crimson.

"There is one more thing," the demon said.

"Yes?"

"I will not hesitate to kill you if you place the border keeper in danger."

Tyn shivered.

"Understood," said Vasethe.

The birds coasted onto a broad balcony near the top of the orange tower and brought the cage to a gentle halt. From this height, the crowds below were rendered invisible. Over the ridge of cliffs encircling the valley, Vasethe could see the wide expanse of the steppe, and the sea beyond. Pricks of shadow marked the sunken ships.

Lfae slid aside the partition that led into the tower. "Second Spear, I will require privacy for the next hour."

"Yes, Res Lfae."

Further partitions, painted with scenes of blue and grey mountains, divided the room into quarters. Lfae gave them a look of distaste and gestured; the screens folded and stacked into a corner. The chambers were sparse but elegant. A circular bed sat like the bud of a flower beneath tents of white gauze, and a long shelf ran along the interior wall, holding a variety of refreshments. Vases of chilled wine, and spiral-shaped confections that smelled of sea salt. Small bowls of crab meat.

"I'll be meeting with a few rulers. I want you to speak to members of their retinues. Gauge the mood. Try to be discreet about Vasethe's affiliation with the border keeper; Buyak will know that he is not part of my retinue, but who knows what other parties may take an interest."

"I'll do my best."

"I don't doubt it." The demon stepped forward and lightly kissed Tyn's forehead. "Stay safe, Upstart."

Tyn nodded respectfully, but her face glowed in the wake of her ruler's affection. Vasethe's heart sped up. He quickly looked away, but not before Lfae saw his expression.

Outside the demon's chambers, the landing echoed with voices. A massive channel of rising water cut through the centre of the tower. Although clear glass panes kept the floors dry, the constant roar muffled and distorted all noise within the space.

Vasethe hurried to catch up to Tyn as she made for a set of descending stairs. "Not fond of heights?"

"What?"

"Back there, in the cage . . ."

"Oh." She pulled a face. "Well, I don't like them, but they won't prevent me from carrying out my duties."

The stairs led to an enclosed passage. The walls were smooth as river stones but undulating and organic, like internal organs. Lines like veins or scales ran beneath the polished surface of the stone. At bends in the passage, warped windowpanes let in the last of the sunlight.

They emerged on floor below. Tyn pointed at an armoured guard skulking around the doorway of another ruler's chamber. "He's one of Kan Moi's attendants," she said. "Would you excuse me for a moment?"

"Sure."

The guard did not have anything interesting to say, nor did the next four dwellers Tyn recognised and approached. Vasethe stayed out of her way, watching lights flicker and gleam in the city around him. He wanted to ask more questions but did not know where to start. When Tyn suggested that they return to Lfae, he stumbled for an excuse.

"Is something bothering you?" she asked.

"Sorry. I'm a little distracted."

"Uh-huh. Try to lighten up, will you? We're supposed to be going to a party."

He forced a smile.

"Well, I guess that's something," she said, unconvinced.

"You seem rather relaxed about all of this."

"I'm good at pretending. Not that this is the ideal realm for deception, but . . ."

Vasethe laughed. The sound echoed strangely in the close, winding passage. "Tell me, why do Lfae and the others call you 'Upstart'?"

Tyn paused and seemed, for the first time, less than certain of herself. She was quiet.

"You don't need to explain if it bothers you."

She waved aside his concern. "It normally takes about eight years to reach the position of Second Spear. I did it in five, so Vehn said I must have seduced Res Lfae. The joke got out. Even though I've been Second Spear for a year now, the name stuck."

"So, you've been in Mkalis for six years?"

"Around six years, yes. It was disorientating at first, so I don't remember much from back then."

Lfae was getting dressed when they returned. The demon had a ridge of scar tissue that extended from their right shoulder to the small of their back. They made no efforts to cover their nudity when Vasethe walked through the door. He muttered an apology and waited out on the balcony while Tyn advised on colour pairings between Lfae's jewellery and dress, and reported back on her conversations with other attendants.

"My meeting was a similar exercise in futility." Lfae sighed. "We can only hope that Midan has been more successful."

Tyn murmured assent.

Vasethe leaned over the balcony outside, his nose filled with the too-sweet smell of honeysuckle and narcissus. He searched the dark skies, egrets rising above the highest tower. The night was filled with the sounds of distant revelry.

"Are you ready, Vasethe? The festivities will begin soon," called Tyn.

He turned and went inside.

Chapter Sixteen

THEY ARRIVED LATE. A throng of gods and demons blocked the entrance to the hall, and the air buzzed with anticipation. In their finery, the rulers reminded Vasethe of a shoal of glittering fish.

He stood to Lfae's left, Tyn to the right, and they waited on the stairs outside. There were no balustrades, and Tyn kept her eyes fixed on the crowd ahead, away from the looming drop beside her. Her expression was grim but resolute; she looked like she would sooner die than admit her discomfort to Lfae. A blindfolded praise singer followed directly behind them, loudly extolling the demon's virtues. The woman had spent the last twenty verses describing Lfae's prowess in battle and gave no sign of slowing. Similar chanters stood in the shadows of the other rulers.

At last the crowd thinned and they were able to see the entrance hall. Solid gold pillars ran in two columns along the length of the room, and rulers milled between them. White-masked servants circled, bearing vases of amber wine, and the smell of food wafted through the air, mingling with perfume and incense. A man sang to the booming of drums. Occasionally, it sounded as though he was screaming.

"Stop looking for her," Lfae said out of the side of their mouth.

Vasethe jumped.

"We are being watched, so try to be less obvious," said the demon, with a hint of exasperation.

The crowd blocking the door dispersed, and they were able to move more freely. Lfae swept towards one of Buyak's servants and selected two drinks served in tiny bronze cups.

"Kan Qi," they called. "I see that you lack a drink."

A shatteringly gorgeous god turned around, hearing his name. His half-naked body was painted with a luminous substance, so that the designs of rabbits and orchids glowed bluish white in the warm light. His praise singer adjusted her position to remain behind him.

"Res Lfae, I see that you have two."

Vasethe tried to mimic Tyn's behaviour, eyes down, face blank, hands folded at the waist. Lfae and Qi began an animated conversation about people and places that he had never heard of, and his attention soon wandered. Guests were pairing up and dancing. A fight broke out but was stopped before it even interrupted Lfae's discussion of High politics.

Qi's only attendant was a cloaked child, who stood still as a stone. Vasethe found that looking at the child was difficult; his eyes drifted away every time he tried, distracted by something else in the room. At long last, the praise singers fell silent. They bowed and left.

"Our host is yet to make an appearance," said Qi.

Lfae shrugged. "His loss. If nothing else, I find the company excellent."

"You flatterer."

Sethe?

Vasethe fought to keep his expression neutral. Relief surged through him.

Tell Lfae to meet me at the base of the rear stairway.

Vasethe glanced at Tyn; he did not know the correct protocol to request Lfae's attention. She was gazing at the dancers, her lips slightly parted.

"Lfae, one of your attendants looks uncomfortable and the other bewitched," said Qi.

Tyn flinched and closed her mouth.

"They are both new to this." The demon sighed and looked at Vasethe. "Well?"

"I believe that someone over there wishes to speak to you," he said under his breath.

"At least that one has sharp eyes." Qi bowed to Lfae, pressing three fingers to his lips. "I hope to see you later?"

"Perhaps I will find your accommodations."

"Perhaps." Qi smiled, and turned to greet a smiling goddess.

"She wants to meet you by the rear staircase," whispered Vasethe.

"She must like you if she's using telepathy to communicate." The demon dropped their cup onto a tray. "This way."

They skirted the dance floor, Lfae fending off the advances of eager admirers. Tyn looked angry, glaring at the ground. Vasethe brushed her hand. She shook her head and walked faster.

Over here.

Vasethe looked towards the voice.

Eris leaned against a gold column. Her hair was pulled back from her face by a band of delicate bronze leaves, and she wore a flowing dress, loose around her legs, high at the neck, her back exposed. The midnight blue fabric shimmered and rippled when she moved, the suggestion of dark waters.

His expression must have amused her, because she smiled. He suddenly found it difficult to breathe.

"Lfae?" she called.

"Ah, there you are," said the demon. "Enjoying the party?"

"Buyak refused my request for passage into the disconnected realm."

Lfae frowned. "Unwise."

She dropped her gaze. "I could scarcely believe that he would dare to say no."

"Cheer up, Midan. Surely, you can force the issue? It's not like you lack ammunition."

She shook her head. "That's just it. It's too obvious. All the coincidence, all the provocation. I feel like he *wants* me to use that ammunition."

"Would you like me to do it?"

"I don't want you to disappear like Kstille did."

"May I remind you that I am higher-ranked than Buyak?"

"But I don't know who his allies are, Lfae. Don't do stupid things on my account."

The demon's expression softened. "Border keeper, I would do almost anything on your account."

Eris grimaced and straightened. "I'm going to get some fresh air. May I borrow an attendant?"

Lfae inclined their head. "If you feel that is wise."

"Sethe." She jerked her head towards the back of the hall.

Guests parted to let her through, their eyes filled with something between fear, hatred, and respect. Vasethe kept to her heels.

The chamber beyond led to a greenhouse, and from there to another balcony. Eris strode past gods murmuring to one another in quiet corners. Lanterns hung between plum trees, and small bells tinkled in the higher branches.

The balcony was unoccupied. Eris slowed. She rested her elbows on the balustrade.

"This is another occasion where I could see the attraction of alcohol."

"Eris?" He hung back, giving her space.

"I thought nothing would change. I stayed in Ahri for four hundred years, and I thought that nothing would change. Now even rulers outside the first hundred are openly opposing me, *sneering* at me . . ."

"Eris." He laid a hand on her arm.

She fell quiet. He leaned on the balustrade beside her.

"I am not sure what to do," she said softly.

"What do you want to do?"

"Snap Buyak's head off." She scowled at the city. "If I don't have their respect, then I will have to earn their fear. The rulers, I mean."

"Because you have to keep them in line?"

She nodded. A dragonfly perched on the edge of the balustrade.

"Left to their own devices, well, the Demonic Wars happen. That much death, it's . . ." She trailed off, lost in old memories. "I won't let it happen again, but I'm just so tired."

"I want to help you."

A smile touched her lips. "You already have."

He snorted. "By letting you suffer a hex I'm too weak to endure. By dragging you into this mess."

She nudged him. "You'd know if I was lying."

"Clearly, it's a subjective truth."

"So stubborn." She rested her head against his arm, and Vasethe's heart skipped a beat.

"You're one to talk," he muttered.

She gazed at the distant steppe. "My son's name was Kol," she said.

Vasethe glanced towards the door.

"It's fine," she said. "Almost everyone here knows what happened, anyway."

"I didn't know you'd had children."

"Hm. Never liked the idea of them, really. But I had lost Yett and I wanted . . . something."

"Who was the father?"

"I'm not sure. Ahri-dweller. More travellers visited back then. As a result, Kol was mortal."

"Oh."

"It felt like he was slipping away from me, every day." Her voice dropped. "He was fourteen when I tried to change the shape of his soul. Make him like me."

"You don't have to—"

"He broke. I splintered him into pieces. Eight pieces."

Eight figures beyond the shadowline.

"So, now you know. Maybe you can write a new dissertation on it."

"I would never do that."

"No?" The moonlight caught on strands of her hair.

He tore his gaze away from her. "We should return to the festivities; you might be missed."

"I doubt it. Let them find me if they want me."

But someone was shouting. Eris frowned. More voices joined in. Vasethe listened, but could not work out what they were yelling.

"Sounds like trouble," said Eris.

He had a sour taste in his mouth. The shouting grew louder.

"Oh, no," he muttered.

"Sethe?"

He took one step, and then another, and then he was running.

Guests had withdrawn towards the edges of the hall, leaving the dance floor empty. Buyak stood opposite Lfae. Tyn was on the ground in the shadow of her ruler. She clutched a broken arm to her chest.

"I was protecting Res Lfae!" she shouted.

The audience muttered.

"I can't lie!" She struggled to her feet. "I can't break the rule."

"Second Spear, hold your tongue." Lfae's voice was sharp.

"Res Lfae, surely you understand that I won't permit a lowly attendant to accost my guests." Buyak's voice had a lilting quality, the timbre clean and smooth. "This dweller's life *is* forfeit. Let us not allow the incident to spoil the whole evening."

"I've gone to war over less, Buyak."

"Her disrespect should not simply be overlooked."

"Stand down, Lfae," Eris murmured. Vasethe had not noticed her beside him. "He's trying to draw you into a fight."

"Please save her." His voice came out oddly flat. "Please. Don't let this happen."

Eris's expression was pained. "It's too risky. I can see what Buyak is trying to do, Sethe. If I get involved—"

"I'm begging you." Despair choked him. "I'll do anything; please, don't let her die again. She's Raisha. Tyn is Raisha."

As soon as he said it, the knowledge became certainty, the realm rules affirming him.

Eris's eyes widened. "You reckless idiot! You had no way of knowing that for certain."

"Please," he whispered.

She glared at him. Then she reached up, pulled off her headband, and tossed it aside. It hit the floor with a clatter.

Her posture changed, shoulders thrown back, chin raised. She broke away from the crowd and strode towards the dance floor. Guests shrank from her as she passed.

"In the presence of the rulers of the first three hundred, I, the border keeper of the shadowline, Custodian of the First Realm, call for a Tribunal of the High for the immediate impeachment of Kan Buyak." Her voice rang clear as crystal. "Heed me."

Lfae's teeth gleamed. "I heed you."

Silence.

"Am I to know what charges you are levelling against me?" asked Buyak.

"Charges can be brought at the trial," Eris said.

"Come now." Buyak raised his hands, his silver eyes glinting. "I would not want to waste the High's time. Let us hear the charge."

Vasethe could sense a trap. Lfae made a sound of warning, but Eris motioned for quiet.

"Border keeper?" Buyak prompted.

She could not back down without losing face. Her reputation was at stake.

"You forged a God Instrument," she said.

Around the hall, there was a collective intake of breath. Then agony laced through Vasethe's throat, and Eris cried out and fell to her knees.

"Lying is not permitted in my realm," Buyak said, his thin lips curling into a smile. "I am innocent of that charge. I'm afraid you are mistaken, border keeper."

"You ... possess a ... God Instrument," she said, through gritted teeth. She cried out as the lie cut into her again. Blood flecked her lips.

"Please stop. Some of the guests might find your discomfort distressing. Res Lfae, for example."

The demon swore at Buyak.

"I'll reach the truth eventually," she panted.

"What truth? Even you cannot hope to survive much more of this. At any rate, the grounds for a Tribunal have not been met. It renders this spectacle a little redundant."

"You built a forge," she said, heedless of the risk, then whimpered.

"Enough. Let's forget this incident," Buyak said. "The night is young and you look lovely, border keeper. Why don't we dance instead?"

He bent to grasp her forearm.

"Get away from her."

Hundreds of curious eyes turned towards Vasethe.

"Isn't it enough that you've humiliated her?" Vasethe spat. "Get away from her."

No one moved. Blood pounded in his head; his vision had narrowed to just Eris and Buyak. His breathing was ragged.

"*More* attendants?" Buyak said with mock incredulity. Scattered laughter.

"Are you another of Lfae's, then?"

Vasethe stayed silent.

"No matter. Your impudence will—"

"He's mine," said Eris. She picked herself up, smoothing her dress. "Before you suggest any more executions."

Buyak's eyes gleamed. All around the hall, guests were whispering. "My apologies, border keeper. I didn't realise that you had a new consort, after all these years."

Lfae took a step towards Buyak, fists clenched. Eris glared at the demon, then turned back to Buyak.

"He is not my consort," she said.

"Then what exactly is your relationship to him?"

"None of your business."

"My apologies," said Buyak, not at all sorry. "It seems I struck a nerve."

"I'll strike more than that, Buyak," Lfae snarled. "You underhanded, sadistic piece of—"

"No, Lfae." Eris was shaking. She drew her head up, although Vasethe could tell she was in pain. "We're leaving."

She swept out of the hall without another word. The crowd's muttering grew ever louder.

"Come on," Lfae told Tyn, throwing a last disgusted

look at Buyak before guiding their attendant towards the door.

Vasethe gazed around, feeling the weight of the room's attention on his shoulders. Buyak's expression was smug, self-assured.

"You know who possesses a God Instrument," Vasethe said, loudly.

The onlookers fell deathly silent, and Lfae paused at the door. A heartbeat. No punishment, no pain. Buyak's face twisted.

"Thought so." Vasethe smiled coldly. He followed Lfae. His footsteps rang on the tiles, and no one spoke.

Chapter Seventeen

HUDDLED IN THE BIRDCAGE, Eris looked battered and defeated. The wind tugged at her loose hair, and her eyelids were half-closed. She seemed smaller, her eyes hollow. Lfae sat beside her with one arm wrapped around her shoulders, either to console her or keep her upright.

"This is my fault," said Tyn.

"Silence, Second Spear."

Lfae's attendant shook her head. Her expression was mutinous, her cheeks flushed with emotion. She clutched her left wrist close to her chest. With every jolt in the flight, she winced. Soundlessly.

"Tyn," Lfae began, troubled, but stopped. "We can talk about it later."

Vasethe held himself apart. His throat ached, but even now Eris was withstanding the hex on his behalf. Just as she always had. The oasis beneath the cage was a well of darkness; he imagined falling into it. High above, the music started up again.

"You still have allies, Midan," said Lfae. "Recover, and then we can decide on our next move."

"I saw," she said. Her voice was scarcely above a whisper, her first words since the party. "The way the rulers looked at me."

"You've come back from worse."

Her eyes drifted closed.

They landed on the balcony of Lfae's quarters. The moment the cage touched the ground, Tyn was on her feet. She knocked into Vasethe as she pushed the door open and stalked across the balcony into the chambers. A second later, he heard a door slam.

"Oh, First's blood," Lfae muttered darkly.

Eris shivered and stood, using the bars of the cage for support.

"They're going to turn on me," she said, and there was fear in her voice. Her breathing emerged shallow. "That's what Buyak intended. He wants them to think I've lost my mind."

"Let them think what they will"—the demon offered her a hand—"and then prove them wrong."

Vasethe stepped out of the way. Lfae guided her inside, and the fire in the grate burst to life. She slumped onto the couch before the flames.

"Vasethe, a word, please," said Lfae, and nodded towards the balcony.

The egrets took to the air in a perfectly synchronized movement, their wings rising and falling as one. Lfae slid the screen shut to prevent Eris from overhearing their conversation.

"Are you hurt?" the demon asked brusquely.

"No."

"In that case, I want you to find Tyn and bring her back here before anything else goes awry."

"What about the border keeper?"

"What about her?"

Vasethe met the demon's eyes. Something in his expression caused Lfae's lips to thin.

"Watch yourself. I'm astonished that Buyak didn't kill you for your impudence tonight. In his position, I might have."

"Eris needs—"

"Who are you to say what she needs?"

He bit his tongue.

"I don't doubt your integrity," said Lfae, with less heat. "However, I've known Midan for close to a thousand years. She trusts me to watch over her."

Vasethe felt the slight but remained silent.

"If there's any danger, I'm better prepared to protect her."

"I'm aware of that."

He stiffened when Lfae placed a hand on his shoulder.

"Vasethe, I understand that you are angry. I do. But I'm not your enemy here. I'm only asking for your help because I don't want to leave her alone while she's vulnerable. You see that, don't you?"

The demon's hand was warm and steady. The last of Vasethe's resistance crumbled and he nodded.

Without the cries of other rulers' attendants, the landing beyond Lfae's chambers felt eerily quiet. Vasethe's instincts guided him; he made for the stairs. Given the choice, Raisha would have moved closer to the ground.

Ropes of reddish lights lit the passages, imbedded in the walls like fat, glowing tapeworms. The floor shone wetly, and the stone's appearance had a liquid quality, slow-melting ice or thick cream. One landing, then another. The wind whistled through the tower's hollow core.

Eris's cry of pain rang loud in Vasethe's memory.

She hadn't flinched when he had poured brandy on her open wounds. The hex that drove him half-mad was little more than an inconvenience to her. And yet, when she lied to Buyak, she had screamed.

The sound of rushing water grew louder. Vasethe emerged from a stairwell to find himself on the lowest level of the tower. A sheet of water gushed over the farthest wall; the lights of other towers blurred and diffused through the liquid partition. The room served as a communal lounge, crowded with low, heavy furniture upholstered in white and gold and mint-green. Thick drapes hung between the couches to create the illusion of privacy, and pale shoots of bamboo grew in porcelain vessels. The light was dim; the braziers had burned down to embers.

Tyn paced like a caged animal. Her boots scuffed the stone, and the knuckles of her right hand were bloody.

"Lfae asked me to find you."

She nodded, although she didn't stop moving. Vasethe leaned against a column. He waited.

"Not yet," she said, under her breath. "I intend to go back but . . . not yet."

"May I see your arm?"

Her steps faltered. She raised her head.

"It must be painful." Vasethe gestured at an ivory-coloured divan. "Please?"

Her forearm was only slightly swollen. He cautiously raised her elbow, lightly pressing on the skin around the bone, testing her responses. She suffered his examination without complaint.

"Clean break," he muttered to himself. He eyed the plants. "Got anything sharp?"

Tyn jerked her right wrist, and a shiv fell from her sleeve into her palm.

"You might as well keep it," she said. "Didn't do me any good."

Vasethe tested the strength of a tender bamboo

sapling. The leaves had only just begun to bud. "You're too hard on yourself."

"I disgraced my ruler." Her shoulders sank. "Are you sure you want to damage Kan Buyak's property?"

The wood gave under her shiv, bleeding sap. He snapped the stem off sharply. "Quite sure."

He cut a swath of rich, soft brocade from the drapes—relishing the sound of the priceless fabric tearing—and fashioned it into a sling. The thick material cushioned his bamboo splints.

"Lfae is worried about you," he said.

"Which is far more than I deserve."

"Isn't that against your code or something?" Vasethe tied the ends of the fabric around her neck. "Questioning the wisdom of your ruler?"

"We don't have a code," she said sourly. "And Res Lfae doesn't demand obsequiousness."

"That's lucky. You might have made a terrible dweller otherwise."

"How would you know?"

"Hm." He straightened. "Just a suspicion."

She moved her arm a little, testing the sling. It appeared to satisfy her. She glanced up. "Thank you."

"Don't mention it."

"I probably shouldn't ask, but—" She sighed. "It makes very little sense to me. Why did she intervene?"

The full weight of Vasethe's guilt pressed upon his shoulders.

I can see what Buyak is trying to do, Sethe.

The words stuck in his throat. "I asked her to."

Tyn stared at him and he looked away, shrinking from her eyes. Eyes that had seemed a little familiar, even though Raisha's had been darker, and Tyn's were larger, but in some inexplicable way they were alike to him. "I didn't consider the consequences at the time," he said.

"You asked the border keeper to save me?"

"I begged. And she suffered for it." He shook himself, and quickly added, "I'm glad she stopped Buyak from hurting you, I just . . . I wish things had turned out differently."

Tyn was still staring at him. "But why would you do that?"

"I was scared Buyak would execute you." He frowned. "Actually, what *did* you do? When I arrived, Lfae was arguing with Buyak."

"I attacked a guest," she said.

"That much I gathered."

"She had a knife, and she lunged towards Res Lfae." Tyn made a frustrated sound. "So, I tried to stop her, and she broke my arm. Like I was nothing. Not even a threat to her."

"A woman?" Vasethe's stomach sank.

"Buyak's attendants escorted her to safety." Tyn's lip curled. "I don't think I even left a scratch on her."

"Did she have white hair?"

"Yes. Tall, very pale, green eyes. Did you see her?"

"Not tonight." He stood up.

"What's wrong?"

"I've got a really bad feeling," he said. "We should return to Lfae."

"Okay." Tyn rose. "I'm sorry for running off; I just—"

"I understand." He smiled uneasily. "You wanted space."

And yet, even as they climbed the stairs, Vasethe's anxiety increased. He needed to talk to Eris; he was missing something. Tyn moved easily despite her arm and eyed him with obvious concern.

"Who is this woman?" she asked. "A ruler?"

"I assume so."

"I think she must hold a minor realm, then. I should be able to identify most of the first three hundred."

Vasethe ground his teeth together. "Maybe."

"If so, she shouldn't pose much of a threat. Especially with Res Lfae protecting the border keeper."

Vasethe could see the logic of her arguments, and yet his instincts still insisted that she was wrong.

"It feels like a setup," he said.

"A setup for what?"

"Something that requires Eris to be weakened." *Or eliminated.* "The shadowline? Maybe someone wants to cross it. Where is the exit for Res Lfae's realm?"

"A few miles outside Demi Anath. Vasethe, slow down."

His mind raced. "We should get her out of here now. If the woman is still in the city, who knows what—"

"Vasethe."

He ground to a halt. "What?"

"I've never seen this passage before."

Her words took a few seconds to sink in. Although the corridor looked no different to him, Tyn had spoken unequivocally. A truth. The smooth, undulating walls radiated coldness.

"Okay," he said. A shiver ran down his spine. "Maybe we took a different path through the tower."

"I don't think so." She ran her fingers over the surface of the wall, distracted. "Some kind of illusion, perhaps. I hope—"

She turned abruptly and retraced her steps. Vasethe followed after her.

They reached the top of the stairs, or rather, the place where stairs should have been. The light vanished beyond the third step, and darkness gathered into an impenetrable barrier.

"What is that?" Vasethe stared dumbly at the wall of

shadow. He took a step toward it, and Tyn caught his wrist.

"Stop," she said.

"But—"

"It's too late. We've already crossed realms."

"What?"

"We've passed out of Buyak's domain." Tyn did not sound afraid. She released his arm. "It was careless of me."

Vasethe's skin crawled. "We crossed without noticing?"

"Yes. Tricked into it." She pressed her lips together. "The real question is why. We should see where the passage leads."

"Do we want to know where it leads?"

"There's no point in staying here; a channel only opens in a single direction. But if we can determine where we are, maybe we can find a way back."

"Always were good in a crisis," he muttered.

"Excuse me?"

"Nothing. You're right, that's all."

She gave him a hard look. He shrugged.

The passage curved and the lights in the walls steadily dimmed, replaced by the glow of far-off daylight. No windows now, and a layer of fine dust covered the floor. It rose in clouds of powder when they walked.

Not dust, Vasethe realized. Ash. The faint smell of

lilies caused his chest to tighten. He paused.

"Is something the matter?" asked Tyn.

"I just had a strange feeling. Like I've forgotten something important."

"Keep it together, okay?"

The daylight grew stronger. When they rounded the next corner, the passage came to a sudden end.

The realm was vast. They stood on a sheer precipice overlooking endless miles of dark hills. Thick mist coiled in the valleys. Nothing alive, nothing growing, nothing that moved but the wind. Peculiar rock formations grew from the murk; sharp, cracked mounds rose from the ground like giant termite hills. The sun was faint through the fog, staining the landscape red.

And ahead of them, a scar in the landscape, was the city. It sprawled over the hillside; close-packed brick houses and soot-stained halls. At the crest of the hill loomed a tiered palace, its high walls rising above the rest of the city.

And everything dead and blackened and still.

"It can't be," breathed Tyn.

"Do you know where we are?"

She turned to him, smiling faintly, as if she expected him to tell her it was all an elaborate joke.

"The Realm of Ghosts," she said. "The 41st. What used to be the domain of the Goddess Fanieq."

Chapter Eighteen

THE OLD ROAD TO the city remained mostly intact. It cut through the hills, straight and level, although the mist made it difficult to see farther than a few feet ahead. The shadows of abandoned wagons and wooden carts emerged from the whiteness, the metal wheels rusted in place, never to move again.

"I've seen this place before," said Vasethe. "I think it's the realm we were trying to reach."

"Why you'd want to come here is beyond me," Tyn replied. She stopped beside a wagon, braced her foot against the boxboard, and snapped off one of the guard rails. She hefted it in her right hand, holding it out in front of her.

"You are sure this is the 41st realm?"

"Certainly looks like it." She swung the pole with her right hand, tracing smooth arcs through the air. "When the border keeper destroyed Addis Hal Rata, this place was closed off to all but the High. Even their channels disappeared after she abdicated to Ahri. No one goes in. No one comes out."

"Except for us."

"Lucky, lucky us." Tyn spun and hit the side of the wagon, hard. Vasethe saw her wince as the force jarred her left arm, but the pole held firm. "We must reach the city before nightfall. If the stories are to be trusted, there's a kind of curfew in place. We don't want to be caught breaking it."

"Caught by who?"

"Fanieq had her dwellers," she said gruffly. "They're still here. In a sense."

The mist dampened Vasethe's clothing and caused the fabric to stick to his skin. The air was mild but curiously stale. Beads of moisture ran down the back of his neck.

They came to a fork in the road and kept straight. Strange rock formations towered over them, rising from the damp ground like spearheads. Huge mud-filled fissures cut across the verges of the road, and slow bubbles rose from the muck. Vasethe, peering closer, noticed what appeared to be thick, trailing weeds growing in the sludge. He tugged the strands free and found himself holding a clump of human hair. Brown and slick, long as his forearm. He dropped it and wiped his hands on his shirt.

The damage to the first buildings was not too severe, although their brickwork had grown spongy with mould and dampness. A mix of ash and sludge choked the gutters. Vasethe kept watch and Tyn searched through the houses for weapons. The sun had sunk below the palace walls, outlining the steep roofs of the city in yellow light, preserving them in amber.

They pressed on, rarely speaking; something about the realm demanded silence. The road widened and the houses grew smaller. Ugly streaks of old soot coated the walls. A fire had gutted whole districts of the city and left only the skeletons of buildings standing. Shattered roof tiles littered the ground, and pieces of broken glass caught the light. In some places, the streets had collapsed into sinkholes, and the subterranean water system was visible: huge rusted pipes, ferrying a trickle of sludge downhill.

The light was fading quickly. With a heavy ceiling of cloud blocking out the moon and stars, night would be pitch dark. Vasethe rubbed his arms. Tyn, only a few steps behind him, was scarcely visible through the grey mist. If he lost sight of her, she might vanish entirely, swallowed up by the city.

"Up there," she said, and pointed to the end of the street.

When he turned around, he saw a wavering orange light through the mist. A lantern, swinging on a post. As they approached, the building behind the light swam into focus: a tall, narrow edifice of dark stone. Unlike its neighbours, it appeared unscathed—the windows were still intact and the roof secure.

He exchanged a sidelong glance with Tyn. "What do you think?"

"I think that we don't have much time to search for an alternative. It looks defensible, at least."

The front door was unlocked, but it took both of them to force it open; the ancient wood had swollen with moisture and fused to the frame. Vasethe took the lantern down from the post.

"I hope we can find something to burn," said Tyn. She shivered. "It would be good to dry our clothes."

The last of the daylight had vanished; everything beyond their sanctuary was invisible. In the pool of wan lantern light, Tyn's tattoos flickered and twisted. A good excuse, the clothing. But they both knew that the lantern was meant to keep the darkness at bay.

"Come on," she said.

Vasethe pulled the door closed behind them and slid the bolt into place. His heart was thumping, although he wasn't sure entirely why. He raised the lantern above his head.

Inside, the building appeared to be a temple. The walls were stained a rich, dark shade of copper, and the roof was high and shadowed. Thousands of gold coins were inset into the varnished floor, arranged in perfect interlocking rings. Malachite statues—three on the right, four on the left—formed a short corridor that led to an altar at the far end of the chamber.

Each statue held a steel bowl in their outstretched hands, filled with oil. Vasethe moved from one to the next and used the lantern to light them. Seven statues. All of the same women in different dress and ornaments, different aspects of the realm's goddess. Warrior, judge, dancer, shepherd, scholar, queen, beggar. The last of them, the shepherd, had lost her face and shoulders, the stone blasted clean away. Her staff remained upright, held by a dismembered hand. He set the lantern at her feet.

"We'll look for the exit from the realm tomorrow," said Tyn. She tried to untie the sling around her neck with one hand. The fabric was sodden. "It's bound to be somewhere within the city, probably near the palace."

"Can I help?"

She nodded. "If you don't mind."

He worked the knot loose. "I didn't think this would need to be waterproof."

The layers of fabric securing the bamboo splints were only mildly damp, so he left them in place.

"Vasethe?" said Tyn.

"Yes?"

"I was wondering . . ." She sat on the edge of the warrior statue's plinth. Her eyes were averted; she toyed with the frayed edge of the splint binding.

"What?"

"No, it's nothing." She swallowed, and shook her head. "Never mind."

She seemed embarrassed, so Vasethe left her alone. He picked up the lantern and set about exploring the rest of the building.

Behind the altar was a small door. Archways stood on either side of it, leading into a curving, windowless passageway. An enormous mural covered the walls of the passage; the painting stretched from one end to the other.

Once, it must have been remarkable. The detail was incredibly fine and deliberate, not a brushstroke wasted. Even now, peeling and chipped and grown over with mould, it demanded attention. On the wall beside the first archway was a string of words written in a red, swirling font, but Vasethe did not recognize the language.

The narrative of the painting began on the left, with an armoured warrior standing below a rippling standard, her shining army spread out on the plains below her. Facing her across the battlefield was a kneeling man clothed in black, his head bowed in surrender or penitence.

The back of his cloak fed into the next scene, where a great festival was underway; people dancing and bow-ing before the throne of the warrior queen. She gazed at the crowds, unsmiling, her eyes seeing beyond them to a storm on the horizon.

Masses of purple clouds roiled, and from them arose a woman with scarlet skin and hair like lightning, her eyes wide and insane, her teeth bared in a hideous snarl. She was naked, and snakes coiled around her bare limbs. Where her feet met the earth, flames burst from the grass.

Now the warrior stood before the gates, her guards arrayed behind her and her sword raised in defiance. Beautiful, glorious. Doomed. The border keeper, grown to the size of a giant, bore down upon her with burning knives, and the city was aflame, people torn apart and bleeding, children howling at the sky, rivers of gore, and only the warrior queen to stand before the onslaught.

"It bothers you, doesn't it?"

He started. Tyn stepped closer, gazing up at the mural.

"It's difficult to reconcile with the story I heard," he admitted. He couldn't stop himself from adding, "The painter had a degree of poetic license, too. Even as Wrengreth, she wouldn't have been indiscriminate."

"Some facts are unassailable," said Tyn.

"Eris never denied that she killed Fanieq. And maybe some other dwellers were caught up in the violence, but this?" He gestured at the wall, willing Tyn to agree with him. "It's exaggeration."

"Maybe. Maybe not. You've seen what remains of the city." Tyn laid her hand over a figure of a crying child, blotting them out. "The truth lies somewhere between the story of the conqueror and the story of the conquered."

She ran her fingers sideways, following the painting to its final image.

The queen lay alone before a broken throne, clasping a wound in her chest. The sun shone upon her, and her expression was fierce and determined. Through a gap in the wall of the palace, she gazed at a silver-leafed grove and a house in the woods.

"There's a second inscription here." Tyn moved to read the writing at the edge of the mural. Vasethe scarcely heard her, staring at the small, painted house.

"Down the hill and into the valley, where the sun cannot shine. Down the hill and into the valley, where the house of bones lies. Queen of Ghosts, where burns your kingdom, Queen of Loss, where burns your heart. Hush, hush, under stone, under water, what secret place you hide. Hush, hush, the witch will hear you breathing. Hush, the witch will know the lie."

And like a switch in his brain, he remembered where he had heard the chant, why he had believed it to be a nursery song.

"She never died," he whispered.

Nialle bent over the cradle, singing softly to her baby. The same words. His memories were so vague and clouded, he could remember asking her about the lullaby, and her laughing—*just something I heard, just a silly little song*—and then nothing. Holes in his past, long stretches of nothing, up until her death.

"What did you say?"

"Fanieq. Eris thought she'd killed her; but what if she was wrong? What if, all along, Fanieq hid in a minor realm and survived?" He squeezed his eyes shut. "No one ever tried to claim the 41st realm, did they? It's still hers."

"You don't know that."

"All of it was meant to drive Eris back into Mkalis." Bile rose in Vasethe's throat. "Fanieq wants revenge."

A loud bang shattered the silence outside the temple. They jumped. A throaty, seesawing screech pierced the air, and the ground trembled.

Tyn caught Vasethe's eye and pressed a finger to her lips.

Something scrabbled at the front door, like a dog trying to claw through the wood. It breathed heavily. In the wavering torchlight, Vasethe could see a pool of oily water forming at the gap beneath the door.

It rammed into the door again.

Tyn crouched silently and picked up her pole. She

pointed at the door behind the altar.

The inner sanctum was colder than the rest of the building. The small, circular room had gilded walls and a drain set into the floor. Tyn shut the door with care and slid the rows of slender bolts into place.

"I don't believe anything will get inside," she whispered. "But if they do, it's best to put a second barrier between us."

Vasethe nodded.

Another shriek. The sound morphed into a disturbing rattle, nails shaken in a rusted pipe.

"There isn't much we can do but wait until morning." Tyn hesitated. "Are you okay?"

"I'm fine," he said.

"Vasethe—"

"Really. You're the one with the broken arm. I'm fine." Vasethe sat, drawing his knees to his chest. Tyn lowered herself to the ground opposite him and rested her pole across her lap.

More banging. It sounded like their visitor had brought friends.

"I have a question I've been meaning to ask you," said Tyn, "but I'm afraid that you'll laugh."

"I won't."

"It's embarrassing."

"Tyn, come on. It's fine."

She took a deep breath. "Did you come to Mkalis to find me?"

There was a moment of silence.

"It's strange," she said, "but I feel like I've known you for years. From the very first time we spoke, I trusted you. Right away, like you were a member of my tribe. And sometimes you say things that make me feel like you understand me better than anybody else."

"I didn't come to find you."

"Oh." Her cheeks flushed. "Of course. I thought it might be a stupid idea. Forget I ever asked."

"I didn't come to find you," he said quietly, "although I wanted to."

She paused.

"Your name was Raisha Amascine, and we attended the same university," he said. "Six years ago, while interviewing Pol merchants for your final paper, you fell sick. The Pol ships had brought a disease into Utyl; you caught it before the situation could be contained. A week later, you were gone."

She looked bewildered. "I was a scholar?"

"One of the best." He smiled. "Linguistics and anthropology. The rectors expected that you would take over the faculty within a decade. I believe you terrified them."

"Huh. Not what I expected." She tugged at her hair, frowning slightly. "Did the disease kill many people?"

"No, just you and three others." He studied the floor. "It was quick. I wasn't able to see you because of the quarantine, but they let us write letters. You told me there was no pain."

He remembered reading that and knowing that she was lying. He remembered the helplessness.

"Then you were gone," he said. "One day there, the next, gone. All I had left were your letters and the sketch of a tattoo you'd designed for me."

"A tattoo?"

"You always said—insisted—I should get one. It was an ongoing joke between us."

"What did I suggest?"

"It's hard to explain, but you modified a proverb in one of the languages we were studying. It translated to 'dog of any master.'" He paused for a moment and traced the word on the ground. Stalling until he could trust himself to speak. "Because you said I could love anyone. That I would do anything, for anyone, if they asked."

"I like it."

He snorted. "Well, you did come up with it."

"Maybe I was smart after all." She nudged him with her boot. "So, what were you to me?"

"Your classmate."

"Oh, come on."

"I don't think I can answer that."

"All right, then, if you want to be difficult: what was I to you?"

He opened his mouth to answer but stopped. Tyn was still smiling, but tears ran down her cheeks.

"The first person I ever fell in love with," he said.

She nodded. "And yet I can't remember any of this. It's all gone."

Her knuckles were bone-white around the pole.

"I've lost something without ever realizing I had it." She laughed. The sound came out harsh. "Doesn't seem fair."

He was about to say *I know,* but didn't. She brushed at her face with one hand.

"It's all in the past now," she said. "I know that. It's not like I would have wanted to return to Ahri, anyway. I just feel strange when listening to you speak, that's all."

There were a thousand things he should say. All the things he never had the chance to tell her, all that she meant to him. There were a thousand things he should say, but none of them were enough.

He reached out and placed a hand on her arm.

She let out a shuddering breath. Her grip around the pole loosened.

The howls of Fanieq's dwellers did not quieten, but the door held firm. They talked a while longer, and the inner sanctum grew comfortably warm. Tyn used her shiv to carve the end of her pole into a sharp point.

As the night wore on, Vasethe fell into a doze, startled awake by louder banging every few minutes. Each time he closed his eyes, details from the mural returned to him. Again and again, the house in the woods, the city on fire and Eris looming over the walls, Eris slumped on the dance floor with Buyak above her, Eris with blood on her lips. Nialle singing over the crib as the face of her child dissolved into ashes.

Chapter Nineteen

HE WOKE WHEN TYN touched his shoulder.

"It's gone quiet," she whispered. "We should get moving."

The flame in their lantern had ebbed to a low burn. Within the sanctum, he could only make out the contours of her face. He shivered.

"Bad dreams?" she asked.

"Yeah." He rubbed his eyes. "Although I guess it's better than no sleep at all."

Most of the fires still burned at the statues' hands. A crack split the front door, and the bolts had almost come free from the wall. Faint morning light shone through the high windows.

"Seems we chose a good place to hide," he said, and walked over to the statue of the dancer. He blew out the flame and lifted the bowl of oil out of the statue's hands.

"Unfortunately, I have a feeling it was chosen for us. Given that it was so nicely signposted." Tyn wandered over. "What are you doing?"

"I like to be prepared." He set the lantern on the

ground, removed the hood, and slowly poured oil into the reservoir at its base.

"Speaking of which"—she held up the now-dry brocade sling—"can you give me a hand with this?"

"No problem."

He slipped the fabric around her arm. She leaned forward to accommodate him, and he tied the knot at her neck.

"How is it feeling?" he asked.

She waved her free hand. "I've had worse."

"Really?"

"I'm a member of Res Lfae's personal guard. It isn't a ceremonial position, you know." She rolled her shoulder cautiously. "Besides, you did a good job binding it."

"Glad to have been of use." He knelt down and replaced the lantern's hood. He straightened. "You must be hungry by now."

"A little. You?"

"I could eat. In Ahri, obviously."

"Oh, right." She sighed. "Well, unfortunately for me, I doubt there's anything edible in this whole blasted—"

She stiffened. In a single fluid motion, she shoved Vasethe behind her, grabbed her spear off the ground, and spun to face the altar.

"You haven't learned, have you?"

Fanieq stepped down from the dais, and her mantle of

long white hair wafted above her shoulders as she walked towards them. She radiated power; it crackled like electricity in her wake. The same woman who had rescued Vasethe in Umbakur, yet her skin had gained a pearlescent sheen, and she wore sleek steel armour, a skirt of silver mail that glittered with diamond studs.

"Must I break every bone in your body?" she asked. "Will that be enough to drive home the lesson?"

Vasethe tried to step around Tyn, but she raised her pole to block him.

"Stay behind me," she said, under her breath. Her gaze never wavered.

"You think that will help?"

The goddess lifted her pale arms to the ceiling. The flames in the statues' hands rippled.

Vasethe slammed into the wall, hitting his head hard. His vision turned white. Through his daze, he heard Tyn cry out; Fanieq had wrenched her broken arm sideways and now held her by the wrist.

"You think that you can fight me?"

Tyn, he thought, and staggered upright. He fumbled for the lantern.

Tyn bared her teeth. She tried to raise her spear, but Fanieq forced her down to her knees.

"You greatly misunderstand the position you are in," she said.

Vasethe swung the lantern at the goddess's back; without turning, Fanieq caught it in her free hand. The metal buckled under her fingers with a sharp crunch. Shards of glass pattered to the ground.

"Run!" Tyn gasped.

"And you"—Fanieq glanced over her shoulder at him—"are even weaker."

The world lurched, and all the air vanished from Vasethe's lungs. He felt as though he was spinning; colours danced over his vision.

Then they were standing inside the throne room.

The roof stretched high overhead, cavernous and domed, and a shaft of light pierced through a ragged hole above the stairs to the throne. Six hooded guards stood to attention at the windows. They did not react to Fanieq's appearance, remaining perfectly still. Beyond the towering, triple-arched windows, the city far below extended into the distance, and the rising sun cast the wreckage in shades of black and pale gold.

Fanieq kicked the spear out of Tyn's hand, and it clattered out of reach over the polished stone floor.

"Get up," she commanded. She sounded slightly out of breath, as if the act of travelling there had winded her. "There's a task I need you to complete."

Tyn lifted her head. Her cheeks had turned bloodless from the pain, but her eyes were hard.

"No, thank you," she said.

Fanieq smiled thinly.

The weight of Tyn's body shattered the window, sending glass cascading out into the void. She didn't scream. She didn't make a sound.

"*Tyn!*"

Vasethe ran across the room. It was pointless; she was gone, but his mind was blank and his body moved on instinct. As he reached the window, two guards grabbed hold of his arms and brought him to a violent stop.

Fanieq approached. Her lips were stained dark red.

"You will be still," she said, "until I tell you otherwise."

Vasethe's body instantly seized up. He struggled, but his limbs refused to obey; he could not move his arms or legs.

"You killed her," he spat.

Fanieq turned from him, wiping her mouth on the back of her hand. She walked over to the windows and gazed down through the broken pane.

"Not this time," she said, and crooked three fingers.

Tyn rose up through the air; her whole body rigid. Relief rushed through Vasethe.

"Are you ready to be cooperative?" Fanieq asked her.

For a moment, nothing. Tyn didn't seem capable of replying; her jaw was locked and her breathing harsh and erratic.

Then she shook her head.

"No. Thank you." She spoke through gritted teeth.

"I'll do it," Vasethe said. "Whatever you want, I'll do it."

"That isn't an option," said Fanieq.

"Then she'll cooperate. She *will*. Tyn, please, don't do this."

She found his eyes and forced a smile.

"Sorry, Vasethe."

"Dead or alive, you'll still be of use," said Fanieq. "Your corpse can fulfill this task equally well."

"Then go ahead and drop me."

"No!" Vasethe strained to free himself.

"This is your last chance," said Fanieq.

"Tyn, please, listen to me," he begged. "If it doesn't matter, then live. Your pride can't be worth more than that. Don't make me lose you a second time, not like this."

She hesitated.

"Well?" asked Fanieq.

Vasethe could not breathe. Tyn closed her eyes and, with the smallest movement of her head, nodded.

The goddess beckoned. "I thought you'd come around."

Tyn drifted back into the room and dropped onto the stone floor. Tiny scratches covered her arms and neck.

She staggered, and Fanieq grasped her wrist, pressing something into the palm of her hand.

"Give this to the border keeper," she said. "You'll find the channel to Buyak's realm through the antechamber at the end of the hall; it comes out at the Jifui Pass. Tell her that I will forge a God Sword before the next sunrise, but the choice of materials is hers."

"You're letting me go?" asked Tyn.

"Either you do as I say, or I carve the message onto your skin and throw your dead body through the channel."

"And Vasethe?"

"He stays here."

Tyn was about to argue, but Vasethe forestalled her.

"It's better that at least one of us gets out." Recklessness struck him. "Go. Warn Eris. And throw that thing into the sea, or crush it with a rock, or—"

The wound on his throat burned with sudden agony, choking him.

"You should know," the goddess told Tyn in a low, dangerous voice, "that he will die if you disobey me."

Vasethe could not speak through the pain, but his eyes were locked on Tyn's, willing her to understand. Willing her to take the opportunity and run. To save herself and to lie to Eris.

"I'll go," she said.

Chapter Twenty

VASETHE KNELT AT THE base of the stairs, a guard on either side of him. The polished floor gleamed like glass, the rich, unbroken stone rippling with the colours of storm clouds.

Fanieq sat upon the throne and played with a dark-haired infant. She rocked the child on her knees, allowing it to tip backwards, dangerously close to falling, and then catching it at the last possible moment. The baby laughed each time.

"You seem nervous," said Fanieq. The child tipped, tipped, and was caught. "Do you think this might belong to you?"

He refused to answer.

She took the baby by the ankle and swung it upside down. It shrieked in delight as she dangled it over the hard stone stairs, but the laughter broke off when she began to swing it from side to side.

"Stop that," said Vasethe.

Fanieq tilted her head to one side.

"Please."

The goddess smiled. One of the guards approached her. She handed the child over and rose to her feet.

"Do you want to know if she is yours?" she asked. "I could tell you. Do you want to claim her from me?"

The baby began to cry. The high-pitched wails echoed through the empty room and out into the city. Through the windows, the sun was already sinking back towards the horizon.

"She certainly isn't yours."

Fanieq laughed. She descended the stairs. "Of course she is."

"You don't own your servants," he muttered.

"No, I meant that quite literally. She is mine. Flesh and blood." She stopped before him and ran a hand over his cheek affectionately. "You still don't understand, do you?"

He pulled his head away. "Understand what?"

As one, the guards drew back their hoods.

"That I've been guiding you every step of the way."

All of the women were pale. While their faces differed, they moved in perfect, graceful unison, their smiles identical. All except for one, whose face had been ravaged, the tissue swollen and crushed, like it had been melted by burning tar. Water ran from her eye sockets and her smile split the skin of her cheeks. Her breathing sounded wet. A single white braid hung over her left shoulder.

A hand touched his right shoulder. He looked up. Nialle stood beside him. Her hair was white as new paper—had it always been that colour?—and her smile mirrored on Fanieq's face. He stared at her, uncomprehending. She was dead. She shouldn't be there.

"After Raisha, I almost gave up on you," said Fanieq.

"What?" He tore his eyes away from Nialle. "What does she have to do with anything?"

Her smile grew wider. "You really didn't find her death suspicious? Didn't think it was a little too sudden? A little too isolated?"

"What are you—"

"I killed her. Poisoned her, in the hope that you would run off to the border keeper for help."

The rule bound him; Vasethe could not rise. Even so, Nialle and the other guard gripped his arms.

"But even after she died, you were happy to let her rot in the ground, weren't you?"

"Shut up!" he snarled.

His throat burned, fierce and hot, and he forgot how to breathe.

"I imagine that the border keeper felt that. A reminder of her deadline."

Through the pain, he saw the goddess walking towards the window.

"It won't work," he gasped. "Whatever you want a God

Sword for, she'll stop you. She's still stronger than you."

"I have no interest in the Sword; that was always Buyak's goal." Fanieq stared out over the misted landscape. She spoke softly. "She's weak where it matters and has lost her old allies. Once she's here, she won't be able to leave. I will hold all the power."

It was Vasethe's turn to laugh. "You think she'll come *here*? To your realm?"

He saw Fanieq clench her fists.

"So, that's why you gave Tyn the Compass." Understanding dawned. "Because you wanted to draw Eris here alone."

"Be quiet," she snapped.

"You think she'll voluntarily walk into your stupid trap? Look, the sun is setting." His smile grew savage. "You thought she'd be here already, didn't you?"

Fanieq strode towards him. "Be *quiet*."

"And even if she comes, what then?" He shook his head. "She's dual-souled. If you kill her, she'll adopt another body. She'll hunt you down."

Fanieq grasped him by the jaw and lifted him into the air. Her eyes were blazing.

"With a Compass, she'll be able to follow you anywhere," Vasethe rasped. He laughed again. "Why would you just hand her your greatest weapon?"

For a moment, Vasethe thought that she might actually kill him. He stared back at her, triumphant, daring her to do it, break his neck, smash his head against the ground, rip out his throat. For the first time, through the mask of her arrogance and poise, he could tell that the goddess was afraid.

"Better start running, Fanieq," he croaked. "You're dead."

Her grip tightened and he cried out. The edges of the throne room turned black. He could hear voices; Nialle said something urgently, but the words were impossible to grasp.

Then Fanieq let go of his throat, and he hit the floor. Cold, sweet air rushed into his lungs.

"She will come." The goddess's words reached his ears from a great distance. "She knows what is at stake. I will see justice done."

Vasethe tried to catch his breath, wheezing. The baby's screaming rang through the room, and his heart boomed.

"Come here."

Fanieq had returned to the windows, her back to him and her face hidden. Against the setting sun, her body was silhouetted in orange light.

"You may move," she said.

The pressure paralyzing his limbs evaporated, but he did not get up immediately. Fanieq said nothing. She simply waited.

He found his feet and crossed the room. A breeze blew through the smashed window, lifting the goddess's hair off her shoulders. The smell of lilies.

"This was my city," she said when he reached the windows. "My heartland. Addis Hal Rata, the Jasper Star. I can still see it as it used to be. I still dream of it."

Beyond the glass, the ruins were endless. Unchanged, as if the fires had died only hours before. The mist curled like smoke.

"She destroyed it for the sake of one dead god." Fanieq turned to look at Vasethe, undisguised loathing written across her face. "Tell me, how could anyone wish to deny me my revenge?"

The crying of the child was the only sound, rising high and piercing through the air. The last rays of the sun dimmed.

"So be it," the goddess said softly. "Her choice is made."

"Yes. It is."

Eris stood in the middle of the throne room, the Compass lying in her palm.

For a second, no one moved. Then, with a terrible wrenching sensation, Vasethe found himself forced onto the throne. Three guards held him in place.

"No!" he shouted.

Sethe, it's okay.

"No, you need to *leave!*" He tried to pull himself free, but the guards only forced him back down.

Eris had the strangest expression on her face. *I can't do that.*

Fanieq grabbed Vasethe's jaw. She held a copper spoon filled with honey to his mouth.

"Give me the Compass," she demanded. Her green eyes burned.

Eris gazed around, taking in the room, the baby, and the women standing around the throne. She seemed calm and a little sad.

"You split your soul," she said.

Fanieq laughed. "Guess who gave me the idea?"

"That's how you could bring the child across the shadowline without my noticing." Eris took a step forward, and Fanieq tensed. "The Compass granted passage for the baby, and you slipped through alongside her."

"Stay where you are." The spoon pressed against Vasethe's upper lip. He could smell the honey, sweet and deadly.

Eris glanced at the woman with the ruined face, the broken fragment of the goddess's soul. "What have you done to yourself, Fanieq?"

"She stepped out of line." Fanieq scowled. "The Compass. Now."

"Release him first."

"It's pointless," Vasethe gasped. "I've been in Mkalis for too long already."

Fanieq slammed his head into the backrest. Lights danced over his eyelids. Eris rushed forward and two guards stepped into her path.

"Please, I just want to send him back to Ahri." Her voice held an edge of desperation. "I'll give you the Compass, but let him go."

The light of the rising moon cut through the hole in the roof, and Eris stood illuminated beneath it. Vasethe could see that she carried no weapons, nothing to protect herself. Self-loathing surged up within him.

With all his strength, he lunged for the spoon.

No!

Fanieq struck him across the face and his nose broke. He swallowed, but there was no sweetness in his mouth. The spoon clattered to the ground; through the red haze covering his vision, Vasethe saw the honey spreading over stone. Out of reach.

Fanieq grasped his shirt and threw him off the throne. He fell down the stairs.

"The Compass, or I kill your whore," she said.

The guards parted, allowing Eris to pass.

"No." His voice came out thick. He scrambled away from her. "Eris, she wants to use your soul for the God Sword."

I know. She dropped down beside him. *When you get to*

Ahri, run. The Ageless are breaking through the shadowline and my wards won't hold.

"She'll kill you." Vasethe grabbed her hand. "Don't do this."

I'm sorry that I was so blind. She pressed her other hand to his chest and smiled, even as tears welled up in her eyes.

"Eris!"

I missed you, Yett.

The throne room vanished.

Chapter Twenty-One

VASETHE EMERGED FROM SLEEP like a drowning man, gasping and desperate. The edges of objects flickered; he caught glimpses of the throne room through the walls of the house. Eris's hand slipped off his chest.

"No!" He put his arms around her shoulders and forced her to sit upright. "Come on, wake up!"

Her forehead was creased in a faint frown, as if she were thinking hard about a problem. She did not react to him. Her head lolled backwards.

"Please, not for me," he said, under his breath. "I never asked for this."

Beyond the house, a sandstorm raged. The air was filled with growling and crunching; he heard the windows in the front room crack. Wind rushed through the bedroom, tasting of salt.

One death in Mkalis, one in Ahri, and her dual soul would not matter.

Vasethe laid Eris down gently, straightening her hair. He gazed at her face. A part of him expected her to wake, but she was still.

"I won't run," he said.

He found his boots and put them on. Every move he made was precise, controlled. Outside the house, something produced a metallic screech. He stood.

There was a knife block in the kitchen, a hunk of heavy blackwood with six slots. He pulled out the blades—paring knives, a boning knife, a cleaver—and tucked them into his belt.

I missed you, Yett.

He shook his head. A god would have been able to protect her. She was mistaken, and if she wasn't, the knowledge was of no use to him now.

Outside, it was difficult to see more than a few steps ahead. Vasethe pushed through the howling wind, shielding his face with one arm. Sand whipped his skin.

All eight Ageless surrounded the yard. The creatures were circling, hovering just above the ground. Their breath rattled. Wards snapped off the fence.

"'Eris' was your mother's name, wasn't it?" he shouted. His voice was torn from his mouth and devoured by the storm. "That's why you came back."

They did not pause in their slow rotation. Their eyes looked through Vasethe, through the walls, straight at Eris.

"She never meant to hurt you!"

A string of coloured beads shattered. Fine glass peppered Vasethe's legs and the wind surged, almost knocking him off his feet.

'The Ageless drew to a halt. A pained shriek cut through the uproar, and the lock on the gate bent backwards like soft clay. The metal snapped and the latch jumped open. The Ageless at the gate—one-legged, skull stripped of flesh, the first—raised its arm and gestured. Vasethe knew that movement; Eris twisted her wrist the same way.

The gate clanged to the ground.

He threw the boning knife. The blade thwacked into the creature's sternum, cracking bone.

The Ageless glided through the gap in the fence, its blank eyes unblinking.

Vasethe pulled another knife, threw it, reached for the next, threw. The blades sank deep into the creature's flesh, but it didn't seem to notice. Its movements remained unhurried. Relentless. It would not be stopped.

Vasethe swore and retreated through the front door, slamming it shut. He dragged his table over to the entrance, flipped it on its side, and wedged it beneath the handle. Through the window he saw the creature approach. It was alone, its brothers waiting beyond the yard.

He backed away to the entrance of the bedroom, fists clenched around the handles of the paring knives. With glacial slowness, the door handle turned, stuck, rose again. Vasethe held his breath.

With a crack, the table split as the door exploded inwards. Pieces of wood flew across the room, and part of the table slammed into the wall. The Ageless drifted past it. The wood warped, carvings distorting into depraved, impossible curves.

Vasethe threw his knives. One missed; the other drove straight into the space where the creature's heart should have been.

He shot a glance over his shoulder. Eris had not moved; still trapped in Mkalis. Her chest rose and fell.

He raised his last knife. The cleaver. The blade was chipped and its edge blunted by centuries of use. Holding it in front of his body with both hands, Vasethe blocked the entrance to the bedroom.

The Ageless's head brushed the lantern and it shattered, the beautiful filigree catches breaking into hundreds of tiny shards, the rose glass evaporating into splinters.

But when the creature reached Vasethe, it paused. Its eyes moved, focusing on the living obstruction before it. There was no curiosity in its gaze, nothing human, no feeling, just pure intent.

He spat at it.

An invisible force drove through his gut. Vasethe hit

the wardrobe and slumped to the floor, blood spraying from his lips. He looked down. A wound gaped across his abdomen.

The Ageless entered the room.

"Wait!" Blood gushed from Vasethe's mouth. He reached for something, anything; his hand closed on a soft object and he threw it at the creature.

The Ageless paused again and stared at the stuffed rabbit on the ground beside it. Then it turned back to Eris.

"Stop," Vasethe murmured.

He was not in pain, and fear was receding from his mind. He only felt cold. The world had grown quieter now, the storm subsiding.

If he had been a god, he would have known how to protect her. He could see a forest in autumn, a waterfall; he could hear far-off music. And her voice. Not her voice. His voice. Midan. Memories he should not have. Eris. Border Keeper, Custodian of the First Realm. The First, who had claimed the realm beyond the shadowline. Why was that important? He was cold, so close. The First, now gone.

Eris.

Vasethe spoke through blood. "I claim Ahri."

Colour and light shot through his mind. The world beyond his body expanded and filled him: the sandstorm and the shadowline, the saltpan, the desert, Raisha's grave, the wetlands, the mountains, forests, cities, ice, oceans, skies, lives, so many lives, a great starscape of souls spreading around him.

He breathed again, blood sharp on his tongue.

"Kol," he whispered. "Die."

The Ageless screamed once, an awful inhuman shriek. Beyond the house, its brothers joined in. Their voices rang out over the desert and merged into a single cry.

Vasethe's eyes shut. His blood spread warm across the floor.

"Heal," he rasped.

His heart stopped.

~

The sun rose above the desert. All was still and quiet and bright.

The storm had vanished. It left behind a small, wrecked house at the end of the tracks, on the Ahri side of the shadowline.

Fragments of broken wards punctuated the yard. Discarded dolls' legs, glossy black feathers. A torn awning hung from the post above the door, hanging on by a few strands of thread.

The front room glittered as the light broke through the windows and the hole where the door had been. Everything was covered by a carpet of glass. Wood splinters littered the floor; the remains of a once-beautiful table lay in pieces. A knife was buried to the hilt in the soft sandstone wall beside the window.

In the bedroom lay two bodies and a battered stuffed rabbit with blood smeared across its ears. The painting on the wall tilted at a dangerous angle, the waterfall cascading sideways.

Vasethe's boots grew warm in the rising heat of the day. He groaned and stirred. The floor beneath him was sticky; his tongue was thick in his mouth. Turning sideways, he retched, then shakily raised his head.

"Eris?" he croaked.

She did not answer.

He dragged himself to the bed, crawling on his hands and knees. His wound had closed, although his clothes were still covered in gore. A perfectly circular scar remained just above his navel.

Eris had not moved, but her frown had faded. Vasethe rested his head on the side of the bed. His gaze travelled to the devastation around him.

It took time. He cleaned the bedroom around Eris first, then swept the front room. The kitchen had escaped largely unscathed; he cleared the mess left by the cracked windows and moved to the yard. He hummed while he worked. In the storeroom, he found a new lock for the gate. When he set it back in its hinges, the latch still stuck.

The sun beat down. Vasethe sighed and pushed back his hair where it fell in front of his eyes. He found his gaze drawn to the saltpan. Beyond the shadowline he could see nothing but white.

He unscrewed the hinges of the gate. The latch would bother him until he fixed it.

Inside the house, a baby started crying.

"Sethe?"

He turned.

Eris stood beneath the ruined awning. Her expression was cautious, her hand half-raised, reaching towards him as if to confirm that he was really there. They stared at one another.

A slow smile spread over Vasethe's face.

The rain fell from the cloudless sky, darkening the sand, cool on her skin.

Acknowledgments

I have been immensely fortunate to work with Tor.com Publishing on *The Border Keeper*. It has been a privilege to collaborate with all of you.

Thank you to Irene Gallo, creative director and publisher, and to Lauren Hougen, production editor. The beautiful cover of this book was the work of Kathleen Jennings and Christine Foltzer.

Thanks to Mordicai Knode, not only for your marketing efforts, but also for producing my first ever fan art. Thanks to Amanda Melfi for your work in pushing this novella on social media. And thanks to Caro Perny for publicity schemes and shouting about crab children.

On the prose side, I am indebted to copyeditor Richard Shealy and proofreader Ingrid Powell.

Thank you to Ruoxi Chen. Ever since you selected this novella from the slush pile, you have buoyed me up with your passion, insight, and enthusiasm. Your edits pushed me to make *The Border Keeper* a better book. I am deeply grateful for everything that you have done for me, and it has been an honor to work with you.

Closer to home, I'd like to thank the Mandela Rhodes

Foundation for the faith that they have shown in me.

Scott H. Andrews, thank you for letting me join the *Beneath Ceaseless Skies* team, and for being so consistently kind and thoughtful. This industry is made better by your quiet dedication and your steadfast adherence to the principle of treating writers with respect.

Thank you to my friends, past and present, specifically to Kaitlin Cunningham and Ruby Parker. Thanks and love, always, to Sabina Stefan.

Emma Kate Laubscher, you are wonderful. Thank you for always making me laugh, and for being the most forcefully enthusiastic proponent of my writing career.

Thank you to my dad for all your support and for regularly asking how the writing is going.

Thank you to Sylvia Hall, my mom and editor, for staying up until the early hours of the morning proofreading this manuscript before the submissions deadline. Without your help, *The Border Keeper* would not exist. I hope to make you proud.

And lastly, thank you to Tessa Hall. My first reader, my genius sister, this one is for you.

About the Author

Photograph by Sylvia Hall

KERSTIN HALL is a writer and editor based in Cape Town, South Africa. She completed her undergraduate studies in journalism at Rhodes University and, as a Mandela Rhodes Scholar, continued with a master's degree at the University of Cape Town. Her short fiction has appeared in *Strange Horizons,* and she is a first reader for *Beneath Ceaseless Skies.* She also enjoys photography and is inspired by the landscapes of South Africa and Namibia.

TOR·COM

Science fiction. Fantasy. The universe.

And related subjects.

*

More than just a publisher's website, *Tor.com* is a venue for **original fiction, comics,** and **discussion** of the entire field of SF and fantasy, in all media and from all sources. Visit our site today — and join the conversation yourself.

CPSIA information can be obtained
at www.ICGtesting.com
Printed in the USA
LVHW041543280220
648531LV00003B/496